Miles to Go

BERYL YOUNG

Wandering Fox Books
An imprint of Heritage House Publishing Company Ltd.
heritagehouse.ca

Cataloguing Information available from Library and Archives Canada

978-1-77203-264-2 (pbk)
978-1-77203-265-9 (epub)

Edited by Lesley Cameron
Proofread by Lenore Hietkamp
Cover and interior design by Setareh Ashrafologhalai

The quote on page iii is from Robert Frost, "Stopping by Woods on a Snowy Evening."

The interior of this book was produced on 100% post-consumer recycled paper, processed chlorine free, and printed with vegetable-based inks.

We acknowledge the financial support of the Government of Canada through the Canada Book Fund (CBF) and the Canada Council for the Arts, and the Province of British Columbia through the British Columbia Arts Council and the Book Publishing Tax Credit.

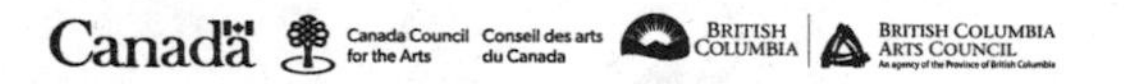

22 21 20 19 18 1 2 3 4 5

Printed in Canada

. . . I have promises to keep,
And miles to go before I sleep.

ROBERT FROST

For my daughter

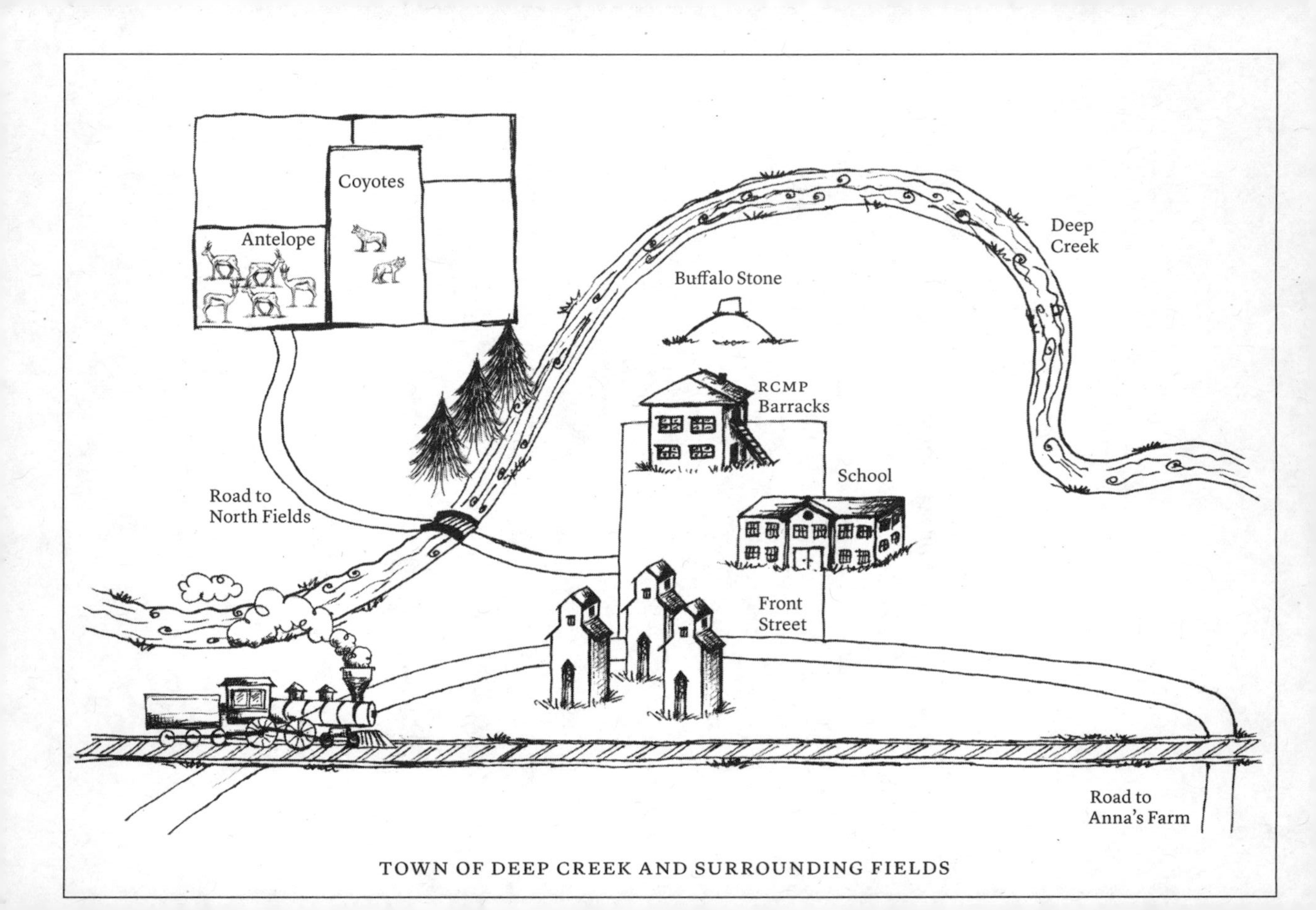

TOWN OF DEEP CREEK AND SURROUNDING FIELDS

Anna

THURSDAY, FEBRUARY 12, 1948

"MEET ME AT recess. Something terrible has happened," I whisper to Maggie as we hang up our coats.

"What is it? Tell me!"

I shake my head. "Recess. The usual place."

For the rest of the morning, the classroom clock seems to be set on slow. Miss Alexander assigns a new project.

"Write about one of our wild prairie animals," she tells us. "Pick a partner and do research on an animal that interests you."

Maggie and I look across at each other. It's agreed. We'll be partners.

Carolyn McAdam tries to get Maggie's attention, but Maggie ignores her.

She rolls her eyes at me. "Got out of that one."

Maggie's smart and quick, and she's always making funny comments in class. Usually I laugh with her, but right now I'm wondering if the recess bell is broken. When it rings at last, I grab my coat and rush to the far end of the playground. I plop myself down beside Maggie on our special bench. She's there first, but in her rush she's forgotten her jacket.

Right away I spill it out. "My mother's having another baby."

Maggie starts to smile, but her smile fades. She looks puzzled. "That's okay, isn't it?" she says, touching my arm.

"Not with my family. Five kids are enough. Mama said she thought I'd feel that way. I should have guessed. She's thin but she has a big tummy. Now the baby's coming in three months."

"Gosh, that's in May," Maggie says.

It's hard for Maggie to understand why I'm upset. Her life is so different to mine, with her proper family and just one younger brother. And she lives in town, so she can walk to school. Not like me. My brothers and I live out in the country on a farm. We have to walk out to the main road to catch the school bus.

"The worst thing is, I'm scared for Mama," I tell Maggie. "Mrs. Covey's the midwife who delivered all of us. She said Lucy should be Mama's last. It would be too hard on Mama to have another baby."

"That's scary," Maggie says.

"What if something happens to Mama? She could die."

Maggie's shivering without her jacket. I put my arm around her.

"I don't understand why Mama would let this happen. Oh, I know how it happens." I smile at Maggie and she smiles back. She has no idea how pretty she is. She hates having to wear glasses.

"Papa sure doesn't feel happy about it. Last night Berny was being goofy at supper and Lucy threw her dish of stew on the floor. Papa started yelling that there were too many damn kids around the house and he had to work his ass off to feed us all."

Maggie looks shocked. I wish she knew what it's like here. Papa says those words—and worse—all the time.

"It feels as though we've always had smelly diapers and crying babies around our place, Maggie. Helen's only four. Lucy's not even two." I can feel the sting of tears behind my eyes. "I don't want people to see us as a poor Polish family, stuck out on the farm with baby after baby coming."

"I don't see you that way, Anna." Maggie smiles sympathetically.

I smile back. That's just what a best friend would say.

Maggie's been my best friend for three years, ever since grade five when she was the new girl in school. She was sitting at her desk fiddling with a pencil and no one was talking to her. I went over and asked where she'd come from. Turned out her father's in the RCMP and her family was transferred here from Regina. First time I'd met anyone whose father was a policeman. It didn't take long for us to be friends.

I can't concentrate on school the rest of the morning. I can feel a thunder cloud heading toward our family.

I found out about the baby two nights ago. The little kids were in bed, and Mama called me over to the couch. "You must know, Anna," she told me. "One more baby comes in May."

Mama could see by my face that I was upset. She patted the couch. "Sit down with me."

I settled close against her. "Are you going to be all right, Mama?"

She smiled at me. "I am lucky with good children. You are my big girl, Anna. We will manage with this baby."

I snuggled close to Mama and her arms wrapped around me like a warm sweater.

One thing I know is that Mama loves all of us. With the light from the kerosene lamp falling in a watery circle on the kitchen table, the thought of another baby didn't feel so bad.

There's nothing I can do about the new baby coming. It's a fact, and I have to accept it. I'll help as much as I can. But I'll never be like Mama and have all those babies. My life will be different.

Maggie

THURSDAY, FEBRUARY 12

THE RCMP BARRACKS sits on a hill at the edge of town. My dad's the sergeant and the officer in charge. He's the most important person in Deep Creek. Even more important than the mayor.

We live in the police barracks. Dad's office is on the main floor. Our apartment is on the top floor, and we need to go up a set of outside stairs to reach it. In the basement are two prison cells and the janitor's room. I know it's weird, but I like it. From my bedroom window I can look right into the tops of the trees.

It's meat loaf and peas for dinner tonight, and Tommy's trying to tell a stupid story about how no one gave him his turn on the swings in the playground. He's doing the usual—separating the food on his plate. Mashed potatoes in one pile, canned green peas rolling around in another, with the lump of meat loaf sitting by itself on the edge of the plate. I know the routine. He'll eat one pile at a time, first the potatoes, then the peas, and finally the meat loaf.

"Stop slouching, Maggie," Mom says. "Sit up straight at the table."

I straighten up. We eat in silence until I tell my news. "Anna's mother's having another baby."

Mom's top lip tightens. "Good heavens, how many does that make?"

"Six when the baby comes," I tell her. "And it's not fair. Anna's the oldest girl and she has to do all the work to help her mother."

"Girls *should* help their mother," Mom says. "You know that."

Tommy's using his fingers to slide peas onto his fork. Mom looks at him with a little smile and doesn't say anything.

"Anna will be all right, Mags," Dad says, giving me one of his lopsided grins. "The Lozowski family can manage their own business."

My dad's the only person in the world who calls me Mags. It's like a secret message between us. As if he's saying, *You're special.*

When Tommy has finished the meat loaf, he gets up and stands beside Dad. He asks for the hundredth time if he can knock on the hard case that holds Dad's gun. We're never allowed to touch Dad's pistol, but he sometimes lets Tommy knock on the holster case. Tommy gets away with it because people think it's cute. It would *not* be cute if a girl my age did it.

"One quick knock, Tommy," Dad says, "and off you go to play."

Tommy knocks, grins at Dad, and is out the door. Mom gets up from the table to take the dishes to the sink. The cotton housedress clings to her skinny legs. It hurts my ears when she scrapes the plates.

I push back my chair. "I have Social Studies homework to do."

"Not before you've helped with the dishes, my girl," Mom says.

"Why doesn't Tommy have to help?"

"Don't you be lazy," Mom answers.

That's so unfair.

I stand beside her to dry the dishes. We don't talk. When we're done, I fling the knives and forks into the metal cutlery tray, throw the tea towel on the counter, and go down the hall to the living room.

My mother likes us to call it the parlour. The cold word suits this room. There's the green brocade chesterfield with petit-point cushions—made by her—in each corner and two stiff chairs. No comfortable seat where a person can curl up with a book.

I prefer my bedroom, where I can lie on my bed and read. I prop up two pillows, cross one leg over the other in the air, and balance the book on my knee. But I'm too restless to read tonight. And I lied about having Socials homework.

I should work on the scarf I'm knitting to give Mom for Mother's Day, but I don't feel like doing anything for her.

I wonder if I even belong in this family. No one else has freckles like me. No one likes to read as much as I do. Apparently I have quite attractive blue eyes, but they're behind glasses, which doesn't help my looks. My bangs are cut so short—courtesy of my mother—they look like stubble in a hayfield.

I decide to go down the hall to hear if my parents are talking about Anna's family. They always talk when they smoke after dinner, and they don't have a clue that I'm in the hall listening to every word.

A match strikes and Mom says, "The man's a brute. No one would breed a cow the way he breeds his wife."

I can hear Dad puff on his cigarette. "Poor guy barely makes a living. His herd's a quarter the size of what most farmers around here run. He's got some problems."

Mom's winding herself up now. "Everyone knows he drinks like a fish. Spends half his time in town and leaves that poor woman to cope with all those kids. Someone should put a stop to it."

I remember once we saw Mr. Lozowski on Front Street. He was shouting and poking his finger in another man's chest. Mom steered me across the street. People in town know Anna's father has a drinking problem. Deep Creek is a small place. Folks know everything here.

Poor Anna.

Anna

MONDAY, MARCH 1

AT LUNCHTIME, MAGGIE gives me half her sandwich and a gingersnap cookie. I used up all the bread making sandwiches for the boys.

"It's terrible around our place," I tell her. "Mama's hardly eating anything but she's getting bigger every day, and she's tired all the time. She wasn't like this with Helen and Lucy."

"She'll be better after this baby's born," Maggie says.

Maggie tosses her apple core in the waste basket. "At least your mother doesn't pick on you. I feel like being mean back to her, but usually I'm not. I'm driving myself crazy knitting a scarf for her."

"I bet she'll like it."

"I'm never sure with her, and I'm not that great at knitting. I keep dropping stitches. The thing's full of holes."

Anna laughs. "They'll let in fresh air, Maggie."

This afternoon we're supposed to be working on our project. Maggie and Jerry keep tossing out wisecracks and making the other kids laugh.

Maggie whispers to me, "Don't you think Jerry's a riot!"

"Sure," I say. "Listen. I've been reading about buffalo. They're the largest mammal in North America. Let's do our project on them. Did you know there used to be millions of buffalo roaming the prairie grasslands? The Cree, the Blackfoot, and the Métis hunted them with bows and arrows for food and clothing. Then the early settlers came bringing horses and guns, and by 1890 the buffalo were hunted almost to extinction. Now only a few thousand are in national parks and reserves."

"It sounds really interesting. The insignia badge on my dad's uniform has a bison on it. Are bison the same as buffalos?" Maggie asks.

"I think you can say either. Let's find out." I pass her the encyclopedia.

We'll both do the research and the writing, but I'll do the final copy of the report because Maggie says my writing is neater. In fact, it is. She rushes through everything, and her writing shows it.

We really like our teacher, Miss Leora Alexander, who is tall and wears long skirts. She has a high forehead and blond hair that curls around her shoulders. She's the kind of woman you'd call graceful, and there aren't many women around town like that!

I want to be a teacher myself. My goal will be to make each of my students feel special. The way Miss Alexander makes me feel.

After school, the bus lets us off at our farm on the south road. The boys race ahead and saddle up horses to go riding. In the house, Mama's asleep in the armchair. She looks like a swollen rag doll. The girls are playing on the floor around her.

Lucy rushes up to hug my legs. She's whimpering, but I don't know what's wrong. She's probably bored. I give her a hug back and wash her dirty face.

I touch Mama's arm. "Why not go upstairs for a proper lie-down?"

Her eyes open and she gives me a tired smile. "Thanks, Anna. I think I will."

I read to the girls until it's time to make supper. Stew again. Lucy makes a fuss about sitting in her high chair, so I hold her on my lap to eat. My school skirt ends up covered with gravy.

Papa's truck drives up as we finish. He digs into his plate of stew and then sends Joe out to milk Dover. I take the girls upstairs to get ready for bed.

When I take them in to kiss Mama goodnight, she's on her back with the covers pulled loosely over her.

Helen says, "Mama's got a baby sleeping in the bump. Can I kiss the baby, Mama?" She bends her dark head and kisses Mama's tummy.

Lucy reaches her arms for me to lift her so she can kiss the baby too. She smacks her lips and says, "Uh-hum." Her only words so far.

"'Night, little girls," Mama says.

Later, when I go in to kiss her goodnight myself, she says, "Thanks, my Anna. I would not manage without you. You are my strong one."

She's wrong. I'm not strong.

I go downstairs and tidy up the kitchen, but I'm too tired to work on the buffalo project.

Maggie

TUESDAY, MARCH 16

AT RECESS, JERRY comes over to talk to me. "Hey, Maggie, so what's it like living in the RCMP barracks?"

"It's neat. There are jail cells in the basement and there's a janitor called Otto. He has a face like a toasted marshmallow."

"Why do you have a janitor?" Ruth asks. She's a friendly girl in our class.

"He cleans the building and feeds the prisoners. We don't always have prisoners in the cells. It's very interesting when we do."

"Weird, more like it," Carolyn says. She juts her chin out when she thinks she's being smart.

Jerry asks, "You ever see the prisoners?"

"Sure. Last year," I say, turning away from Carolyn, "I snuck down the inside stairs to get a look at one."

The kids stare at me.

"I did! I got close and peeked around the corner. I saw the guy. He had sneaky eyes and dark stubble on his face."

Jerry edges closer. "What happened?"

"Well, I guess he was surprised to see a girl standing there. He looked right at me and pointed his finger like a gun and went 'BANG.' I got out of there fast."

The girls look at each other. Jerry's eyebrows slide up.

I shrug. "You get used to living on top of criminals."

"Wow!" Carolyn says.

Anna grins at me, her brown eyes sparkling as she flips her braids with the back of her hand.

After the bell, we walk behind the lot where the school bus parks. The driver's gone to the office and the bus kids are hanging around waiting. Anna's big brother, who's in high school, is there, and her younger brother, Berny, is joking around with the other kids.

Anna and I sit down on the bench at the back where we can talk.

"I wish you lived in town, Anna. We could get together after school and on weekends."

"I wish that too."

"My grandmother's coming to stay with us soon," I tell her.

"Lucky you."

"She's fun to be with. She always laughs at my jokes."

"Is she really old?"

"I guess so. She has wrinkles on her face and brown spots on the back of her hands."

Anna laughs. "Freckles, like you!"

"She has white hair and wears it swirled on top of her head with a silver clip at the back."

Anna smiles at me. "I like hearing about her. Our grandparents are in Poland. Mama and Papa said goodbye to them forever when they emigrated to Canada."

"Gram's the only grandparent I see. Mom's parents live in England."

The bus driver comes out of the school and calls, "Hop in, kids! We're late." Anna waves as she boards the bus with the others.

I take my usual route home, walking along Third Avenue, across Maple, and up Fourth. The pioneers who settled here in Deep Creek kept it simple. The streets that run east to west are named after trees—Aspen, Maple, Birch, Alder, and Cottonwood. The avenues run north to south—First, Second, Third, Fourth, and Fifth. Then there's Front Street, which is the main street by the railway tracks.

I'm still enjoying the attention I got telling the kids about the prisoner. No one has a story quite like that, even though Ruth's mother was once in a bank when it was robbed.

I climb the outside stairs to our apartment. Mom's waiting at the door. "Why do you dawdle on the day you have your piano lesson?"

I choose not to answer, grab my music books, and rush out the door again. Mrs. Dougherty's house is the other side of town, and she gets snippy if I'm two minutes late.

I've taken piano lessons for four years, and here's why I hate it. First of all, Mom makes me get up at six-thirty every morning and practise until seven. The upright piano with its dark polished wood sits like a monster waiting for me in the living room. The row of ivory keys are the monster's giant teeth. I have to sit on the hard piano bench and try to concentrate even before breakfast.

I believe a person's fingers need juice and toast before they can move over the keys. Toast with lots of jam.

"Back straight," Mom reminds me.

The other reason I don't like the piano is that my teacher, Mrs. Dougherty, never smiles or says, "Well done."

Today she goes on again about keeping my fingers bent a certain way. "Fingers poised over the keys," she says sharply.

A *very* weird word. Poised. Like she's saying "poisoned over the keys." The next thing I know, Mrs. Dougherty is hitting my knuckles with a ruler. The metal part! There are red marks on my knuckles. How dare she hit me!

When the lesson is over, I don't say goodbye. I rush home to tell Mom what Mrs. Dougherty has done.

oooooo

MOM LOOKS UP from stirring soup on the stove. "Maggie, I just don't believe that. Mrs. Dougherty is a lovely person. I see her all the time in our bridge group."

"But it's true, Mom. She hit my hands with a ruler. Look at them!"

Mom gives a quick look and shakes her head. Of course, the red marks have gone.

"Why would you lie about that, Maggie?" Her lips are tight. "It's a struggle every day to get you out of bed to practise."

She turns away and starts drying a saucepan. Her elbows stick out like chicken bones. "Now you're trying to get out of piano lessons by telling a lie about your teacher."

Why doesn't she believe me? Why can't she take my side? I plan to tell Dad about being hit by the ruler, but when I think about it later I decide not to. He never makes trouble with Mom. He'd say, "Don't worry about it, Mags."

From now on I'll remember to keep my fingers poised, poised, poised, trying to make them like Mrs. Dougherty's witchy claws. In addition, I decide to hate her. And also my mother. Hate them both. Big time.

I'm not knitting anymore on that scarf. I get my book. I'm sitting reading on the chesterfield when Tommy comes into the room.

"Look at these muscles," he says, wandering over to me. He pulls up his sleeve and flexes his arm.

"I don't see any muscles. Just your scrawny arm."

"See that muscle there?" He waves his arm in front of my book.

I push him away. "Get your puny arm out of my face."

"My arms aren't puny. I'm strong for my age." He marches around the room, punching an imaginary foe.

"No, you're *not*!" I yell. "You're a weakling. Not only that, you're short for your age!"

I turn back to my book, but Tommy's red face is coming toward me. Breathing hard, he pummels me with both fists. My glasses are knocked sideways.

"Stop it, you shrimp!" I shout.

Tommy leans his face in close and spits. The wet glob of spit lands on my cheek. I reach out, full of rage, and shove him as hard as I can. He falls, and his forehead hits the edge of the coffee table.

"Mom!" Tommy screams so loudly it scares me.

Mom hurries in from the kitchen. "What happened here?"

"She pushed me!" Tommy yells.

To my horror, there's blood on Tommy's forehead.

"Come into the kitchen, Tommy." Mom leads him away. "Maggie, get the first aid kit."

I run to get the box from the shelf in the bathroom and put it on the kitchen table beside Mom.

"Out!" she says to me, pointing to the door. "Your father will talk to you later."

It seems like a long wait in my room until I'm called for supper. At the table, Tommy has a small bandage on his forehead. He looks at me like I'm a criminal. He looks at Mom like he's a wounded calf.

Dad's eyes go from one to the other of us. "What's going on here, you two?"

"He asked for it, Dad. He spat at me!"

"She called me a shrimp!" Tommy yells.

"What nonsense," Dad says. "You two better learn to get along. You live in the same house and we need some peace around here."

"Make him leave me alone, Dad," I say.

"Tommy, you do bait your sister. I don't want you to do it anymore. But, Mags, you're almost thirteen. Tommy's just five. You pushed your brother so hard he's cut his head!"

"Sorry." I'm almost sorry.

"Off to your rooms, both of you, right after supper," Mom says.

"What? You know I always go to bed later than Tommy."

"Why do you talk back to everything I say?" Mom looks furious.

"I say what's true."

"What's true, my girl, is that you are going to your room this minute!"

On my way down the hall, I hear her say, "I don't know why that girl's so snippy all the time. She's like a spark looking for kindling."

Like it or lump it, Mom. That's me.

TUESDAY, MARCH 16

MRS. COVEY IS sitting in the kitchen with Mama when I get home from school. She's our closest neighbour and has three children under seven. I always feel badly about her middle boy who has a club foot.

"Hello, dear," Mama says. "Pour yourself a cup of tea and fill the kettle for more, will you?"

Lucy and Helen are playing with our cat on the carpet. Helen's named the cat Boo. I take my tea and sit beside them.

I hear Mrs. Covey ask Mama where Papa is.

"Joseph's in Stoddart right now, selling cows," Mama says.

"That's hard for you, Isabella. Joseph should be around more."

Mama pours more tea. "He does his best for us."

She always stands up for Papa. But he's away too often. As well as his trips to the big city, he's in Deep Creek all the time—and that's not selling cows. He comes home smelling of beer.

Mrs. Covey's a good friend to Mama, and she's delivered lots of babies in the neighbourhood, but she's nosy. I think she asks too many questions.

When Mrs. Covey's leaving, she asks me to come with her. We walk on the path beside the creek that's lined with trees.

Mrs. Covey looks serious. "Anna, I hope your father's planning to be around when this baby comes."

"I'm sure he will be."

I'm not sure at all, but I won't tell her that.

"Come and get me as soon as your mother goes into labour. This baby could arrive quickly. My John will stay with our children when I'm needed."

"I will."

"Your mother had a hard delivery last time with Lucy."

"I know."

I guess I look alarmed, because Mrs. Covey says, "We'll see your mother through. Just let me know when her labour starts."

oooooo

WHEN WE'RE MAKING supper, I ask Mama why Papa has to be in town so much.

"Your father's a good man," she says, "but he needs male company now and then. To take his mind off his troubles."

"Are *we* his troubles?" I ask.

"No, he loves his family. He must make money to keep us all."

"I wish he'd help you more, Mama. He could take the girls when I'm at school and give you a rest. He could fix the broken door on the outhouse, too."

"Papa is doing his best, Anna," Mama says.

Will my father's best be good enough?

Maggie

SATURDAY, MARCH 27, AND SUNDAY, MARCH 28

ON MY BEDROOM dresser I have a picture of my dad in his scarlet tunic and wide Stetson hat. He's even more handsome than Clark Gable in *Gone with the Wind*.

It's the Royal Canadian Mounted Police who catch the criminals in Canada. Everyone says that the Mounties always get their man, and I guess they do. I asked my dad if he'd ever had to shoot anyone, and he said, "Luckily, Mags, I've never had to. I hope I never do."

There's a late frost and a thick snowfall today, and Mom sends Tommy and me outside in our winter clothes. We race to stamp on the ice patches, and the ice cracks like breaking glass. Cold air stings my nose. I blow out long puffs, pretending to hold a cigarette. My breath hangs like milky smoke in the heavy air.

We get the flattened cardboard we've stashed under the side stairs. We line it up at the top of the steep slope and slide down, bumping with a smack into the caragana hedge at the bottom. The bump sends icy snow as sharp as pin pricks into my face.

When we climb back up near the front of the barracks, Dad's secretary, May, is at the door. "Looks like fun!" she calls out to us.

Just then we hear the crunch of car tires on the driveway and see Dad drive up with another policeman. They help a man wearing overalls out from the back seat. His head is down. Snow lands on the handcuffs around his wrists. He shuffles along, as if he's too tired to put one foot in front of another. May scurries back inside.

"For sure Dad's going to lock the guy up," Tommy says.

"He doesn't seem drunk," I say. "Wonder what he did?"

After supper, I'm spying from the hall while my parents smoke at the kitchen table. I hear Dad saying to Mom, "I feel sorry for the poor fellow. Apparently he was so depressed he killed his wife and baby."

I'm shocked. What kind of a person would kill a baby? It's the worst thing anyone could do.

oooooo

IN THE MORNING, I'm still thinking about the prisoner. I'd like to get a look at him. There might be something in his face to show me how he could do such a thing.

I sit in my room, trying to finish the scarf for Mom. My knitting isn't getting any neater. Some of the holes where I dropped stitches are so big you can poke three fingers through them.

The house is quiet, and I figure it's a good time to see the prisoner. I go down the stairs to the basement and stop beside the cells. It's a shock to hear the prisoner crying. Not just crying, but sobbing. I stand there listening. It's the first time in my life I've heard a grown man cry.

Then Otto comes along the hall, carrying a tray with the man's lunch, and I hear him slide the tray along the floor under the bars.

"You eat now. Good food," he says in his thick voice.

I'm behind the hall, so Otto doesn't see me, but I've missed my chance to see the prisoner. Crying like that, he sounds so sad. Would someone who murders a baby feel terrible about what they've done? Dad says the man was depressed. If you're depressed, does it mean you can't control what you do? If you can't control what you do, are you still to blame? I don't know any of the answers.

When I come back into the kitchen, Mom is ironing Dad's shirts. "What were you doing down there, Maggie?"

"I wanted to get a look at the prisoner."

"You know the basement's out of bounds. Don't let me catch you going there again."

Then Mom sighs. "What's wrong with you that you'd want to look at a prisoner anyway? Tommy would never sneak down like that."

"Well, I guess he's the prince and I'm the ugly stepsister."

"I'm tired of that kind of talk, Maggie." She stubs her cigarette out in the ashtray.

I feel like the ugly stepsister, so I might as well say it. "Sometimes I think I don't even belong in this family."

"Don't be ridiculous. Of course you belong with us."

I go to my room and lie on my bed. When you think about it, "You belong with us" could mean anything. Like, you belong here because we adopted you? Not necessarily because I gave birth to you. That kind of statement makes me wonder even more if I was adopted.

I know Tommy's not adopted. He came along seven years after me and I remember him as a baby, especially the crying and the way Mom adored him.

I bicycle my legs in the air, building up my muscles, then lie back on the pillows. I like to imagine a story about my *real* mother. She is an exceptionally warm person with light freckles across the top of her nose, like me. She had a good-looking boyfriend in high school. It was a shame when she found out she was going to have a baby. Maybe the boy's parents disapproved of her because she came from a poor family. She's the tender, maternal type, but keeping a baby would have interfered with her dream of becoming a nurse. So she had to give me up. She was heartbroken and cried for weeks. Deep inside I have a feeling she still thinks of me. She would be upset to know that I ended up with this cold, mean person for a mother.

I shake my head. There must be a devil in me to make up a story like that.

About the only thing I can look forward to is Gram's visit in a week. After Gramps died, she moved from the farm into town, not Deep Creek but not far away in Tumbrill. She often comes to stay for a few days.

This time when she's with us I'll ask her if I'm adopted. I'll promise not to say anything to my parents, although that may be a hard promise to keep.

Anna

MONDAY, APRIL 5

WE'RE EATING OUR lunch in the lunchroom.

"Bet you're excited about your grandmother coming to stay, Maggie."

"Mom says she'll be having treatments at the hospital."

"Why does she need treatments?"

"I don't know. I don't think it's anything serious."

I hope Maggie's right. *Treatments* doesn't sound good to me.

Lunch is over and we go back to the classroom. I wish I could spend more time here in Miss Alexander's peaceful room. Above the blackboard she's put posters of famous places around the world. I'd like to go to those places some day.

Miss Alexander almost never raises her voice, not even when the boys are fooling around. We all know that when she gives us a test, she wants us to pass. I'm taking a mental note of everything Miss Alexander does for when I'm a teacher.

But I can't stay in school all the time. I have to get back to my life on the farm.

oooooo

MAMA'S AT THE stove making soup when I get home. She's huge these days. You'd think by her size the baby was due any day, but there's still more than a month to go.

I tell Mama to sit down, and I take over chopping the carrots and potatoes. The girls are fussy and whiny around us while Mama sits with both hands resting on her stomach. She can't seem to concentrate on anything except this new baby growing inside her.

Papa's away in town. He's just returned from selling cattle in Stoddart, something he does three times a year. The first thing he does when he gets back is head into Deep Creek. He has money to buy groceries for us and drink for himself.

The boys are quiet at dinner. I look at Joe. "I heard from a girl on the bus that you've got a girlfriend at school."

Joe grunts, his face still down at the soup bowl.

"Baseball season's coming up, Berny. Are you playing first base again this year?"

"Yep," Berny answers.

That's it for conversation around our table. Lucy's rubbing her eyes, and Mama says, "Looks like someone's tired. Let's put our girls to bed."

Berny gets up to take the soup bowls to the sink while Mama and I lead the girls upstairs. Just as we've got them settled, I hear the door open.

Papa comes noisily up the stairs to their room. He's weaving around and mumbling, and he smells of liquor. I hate that stink.

"Hey, liddle girls." He tucks Helen in and gives Lucy a kiss and says, "*Dobry wieczor, ptaszek.*" He calls Lucy his little bird.

Papa's never mean when he's drunk. He's just kind of clumsy and slow. I don't mean he's not smart, because he is. He just never learned to speak English very well.

Papa used to be good-looking, but he hasn't shaved and he's still in his work overalls. There's a space where he had a front tooth pulled because he couldn't afford to have the cavity filled. He said it was more important for us to have our teeth fixed.

Papa puts his arm around Mama and leads her to bed. I go back down to the kitchen to do the dishes.

Maggie

WEDNESDAY, APRIL 7,
AND THURSDAY, APRIL 8

GRAM IS TIRED. Dad has to take her arm to help her up the steps to our place.

At supper, Tommy sits at the table, hogging the conversation. I feel guilty seeing the red mark on his forehead, but it's irritating when he babbles on and on.

When Gram comes to stay with us, she always sleeps in my bed and I sleep on the pull-out chesterfield in the living room. Tonight Gram goes to bed early. I sit on the edge of the bed beside her.

"How are things with you, my girl?" she says, propping up the pillows behind her. Her silky white hair drifts over the white pillowcase. It looks as though she's sleeping on a cloud.

"I'm fine," I say. "School's good. Tommy's still a brat."

Gram laughs her soft laugh. "He's bound to grow up. All little brothers do."

"He bugs me. Interrupts what I'm doing and gets mad when I don't want him around."

"Maybe it would help if you did a few things with him. You're his older sister."

"I'd rather have an older sister myself. We could have fun doing things together."

Gram looks across to the top of my dresser. "I see your china bluebird sitting there."

I nod. "Place of honour, Gram, ever since you gave it to me. Remember when we saw my first real bluebird? It was sitting on the fencepost near the road into the farm."

"Do you remember what I said?"

"You said, 'Isn't that the brightest blue in the world?' And it is!"

I show Gram the scarf I'm knitting. "I'm making it for Mom for Mother's Day. I don't know if she'll wear it."

Gram smiles at me. "Remember to pick up the stitches you drop."

"It's way too late for that, Gram," I tell her, laughing.

Gram shifts on the bed as though she's trying to get comfortable. I almost ask if I'm adopted but decide not to. I sit there quietly, and the next thing I know she's asleep.

I tiptoe out of the room and wander around the living room, then sit in the armchair, swinging my feet in the air.

Mom comes in with a women's magazine and sits down on the chesterfield.

"Where's Dad?" I ask.

"He's down in the office talking to Otto. Have you done your homework?"

"Yes. Did it at school."

Mom frowns at me. "Stop twirling your feet. Find your book and read it. What's the matter with you tonight, Maggie?"

"I'm thinking about Gram," I say.

"Just sitting there thinking? Aren't you the strange one."

I go to the bookcase in the hall to get my book. Does Mom mean I'm strange because I'm different from everyone else in the family? Well, it's true, I am different. Most kids would love their mother and their little brother. I don't. At least, not in the wholehearted way I should.

Maybe *this* is the moment. My knees are shaky as I get up and stand in front of Mom.

"Yes?" she says.

Now or never.

"Mom, what do you mean I'm a strange one? Do you mean I'm different from all of you?"

"What on earth are you on about, Maggie?"

I stare at the floor. "Sometimes I feel as though I come from another family."

It seems to me she pauses before she answers me. "Don't be silly. Of course you don't."

Mom's not looking me in the eye.

"It's one thing after another with you, isn't it?" She waves at the door. "Go outside and bring Tommy in, please. It's time both of you were in bed."

"You know I go to bed way later than Tommy."

"Do you have to argue with everything I say?"

"Mom, I'm older than Tommy. We don't go to bed at the same time."

"Go and get him, and both of you get into your beds, right now." She turns back to her magazine.

"I can't go to bed, Mom. You're sitting on the chesterfield which happens to be my bed!"

"Don't sass me, Maggie." She gets up and walks out.

I swear, the next chance I get I'll ask Gram if I'm adopted. She'll look me in the eye and tell me the truth.

••••••

WHEN I COME home from school the next day, Mom tells me Gram's been in the hospital all day for treatments. I rush into the living room and sit down beside her on the chesterfield. She's that comfortable kind of person. When you sit close to Gram you can sort of melt right into her.

Her voice is soft. "Maggie, do you remember visiting the farm and Gramps talking to you about the Saskatchewan hills?"

"I do. I remember Gramps in his straw hat taking me out to the field and pointing to the horizon. 'Never let anyone tell you this land is flat,' he said. 'People who say the prairies are flat don't know a thing.' I do remember that."

"I've been thinking about those hills," Gram says. "They're all shades of blue, aren't they. Pale against the sky and then they get darker and deeper at the horizon."

"I used to think they looked like a watercolour painting."

"It was in that field your grandfather had a heart attack."

"I was ten and I was so sad."

"I'm glad that those hills were the last thing he saw."

I look at Gram. Her eyes are on the sky outside the window, and there's a strange look on her face.

"Gram, are you sick?"

"Well, my love," she says, turning to me and reaching to hold my hand, "seems I might have a small growth in my stomach. Don't you worry."

My chest starts to feel tight. "That's terrible, Gram."

"Oh, Maggie, this is part of growing old." She smiles gently at me. "I'm old, but I'm tough. I'll be around for a while."

I squeeze her hand and I believe her. I need to believe she'll be around forever.

No chance to ask if I'm adopted.

Anna

WEDNESDAY, APRIL 14

I'M ASLEEP WHEN Papa shakes me in the middle of the night.

"Wake up, Anna. Mama has the baby now. You must help."

It's then I hear the baby's cry. The baby has come! I rush into the bedroom and see Mama lying with her eyes closed. The kerosene lamp on the dresser is lit and I can see blood on the sheets around her. Papa picks up the baby with the cord still attached. I sit on the bed and he puts the baby in my arms. It's a girl, and she's so tiny. Her dark eyebrows are two perfect arcs over her eyelids. She's crying steadily now.

Papa goes down to the kitchen and comes back with a kitchen knife to cut the cord. He ties it with string, then wipes the blood off the baby with a towel. The baby has stopped crying, and I hold her up so Mama can see. Mama looks at the baby, but only for a moment, then closes her eyes again. Even in the dim light from the lamp I can see that Mama's face is pale.

"Stay with Mama. I go for Mrs. Covey," Dad says on his way downstairs. I hear the kitchen door bang and his truck start up.

I wrap the baby in a clean towel and try to put her in Mama's arms, but Mama is sleeping and can't hold her. I sit on the bed beside Mama, holding the baby. The baby is very still. I put my face up to hers and feel soft little breaths. She's alive.

"Papa will be back with Mrs. Covey soon," I say to Mama. She opens her eyes and looks at me.

Her voice is so faint I have to lean close to hear. "Take care of the baby, my Anna." Her eyes lock into mine.

"I will, Mama. I promise," I whisper.

I know Mama hears me, because she sighs and goes back to sleep. I sit beside her holding the baby for a long time. Everyone else in the house is asleep. The air is still, with the lonely feeling of a house when you're the only one awake. You might be the only person awake in the whole world.

At last I hear Papa come in. He brings Mrs. Covey into the bedroom. She looks at the baby and smiles. Then she bends over Mama.

Mrs. Covey isn't smiling when she looks up. "She's gone. Your mother's gone."

My mother's gone? Does she mean Mama has died? I hear Papa's heavy breaths behind me.

"Your mother lost too much blood and slipped away," Mrs. Covey says. Her eyes are gentle when she looks at me. "Take the baby downstairs and light the fire. I need to take care of your mother."

oooooo

PAPA LOOKS STUNNED and doesn't say anything as he gets wood and builds a fire in the stove. I sit at the kitchen table with the sleeping baby in my arms.

Something momentous has happened. Mama is no longer here on this earth. Her body is upstairs in that dark room, but she's not there. My chest feels as though it's being squeezed. Is this the pain I'll feel for the rest of my life?

I look down at the baby. She's so light, so helpless with no mother to keep her safe. I hold her tighter.

Then Papa scares me by putting his head down on the table and starting to moan. "I've lost her. Mama has left me with six children. I cannot do it, Anna."

"It will be all right, Papa," I tell him. "I promised Mama I'd look after the baby."

He gets up and finds a bottle of whiskey in the cupboard and starts to drink right out of the bottle.

Mrs. Covey comes down and says she'll call the priest and the undertaker from her home phone. It's starting to get light when Papa drives her home. The baby sleeps on, breathing so softly. I sit in the kitchen, my legs too heavy to move. I think of all the things I have to do. I must remind Joe to milk Dover so there will be milk for the baby. And have Papa bring down the wooden cradle from the attic.

The morning sun streams through the dust on the window and makes everything that happened in the night seem unreal.

◦◦◦◦◦◦

THE BOYS ARE up and the girls too. They're surprised to see the baby, but they sit quietly, the girls not understanding when I tell them that Mama is dead.

"You mean Mama is sleeping?" Helen asks.

"Oh, Helen," I say, "being dead is different. It means she won't wake up."

I see the dawn of fear in Helen's eyes. I don't know how to help her.

Joe goes out to milk the cow, and I let Berny hold the baby. His eyes are red and his nose runs, but he doesn't let go of the baby to wipe at it.

I cook porridge for everyone. We're still sitting at the table at ten o'clock when the priest and the undertaker come in, both of them dressed in sombre dark suits.

Then the night seems real.

The priest looks around the table and says, "You must come upstairs to say goodbye to your mother."

Papa picks up Lucy, and we go into the bedroom. Mrs. Covey has folded Mama's hands over her chest. Her lovely long fingers are pale and limp. I touch her hands and oh, they're so cold.

The girls are frightened and crying. Berny's sobbing, but Papa and Joe don't cry. I don't cry, either. I have to hold the baby in one arm and lift Helen so she can kiss her mother's cheek. No one speaks; the air in the room is heavy.

The priest makes the sign of the cross over Mama and asks God to bless her and take her into the Kingdom of Heaven. Then he pats each of us on the head and says, "Be good children and honour your mother."

They put Mama on a stretcher and carry her to the long, black hearse and drive away. The baby starts to cry.

Maggie

FRIDAY, APRIL 16,
AND SATURDAY, APRIL 17

ANNA HASN'T BEEN at school for two days. Both mornings I wait in the yard for the school bus, but none of the Lozowski kids are on it. Anna's family has no phone. My head is buzzing with worry.

When the bell goes, Miss Alexander stands up straighter than usual at the front of the room. She's not smiling.

"Class," she says, "I have a sad announcement." My heart starts hammering in my chest. It *is* Anna. She must have had an accident.

"I'm sorry to tell you that Anna's mother died two days ago."

There's not a sound in the classroom. From far away I hear Miss Alexander's voice.

"The baby was born early, and the birth was too hard on Anna's mother. Anna will stay at home to look after the new baby and her sisters. She won't be coming back to school. Her brothers will be back next week."

I feel shaky and pull my sweater tighter. Miss Alexander tells us to get our readers and do silent reading until recess. After the bell rings, I wait behind while the others stream into the hall.

I go up to Miss Alexander's desk. "Is the baby a boy or a girl?" I ask.

"It's a little girl, Maggie." She looks at me, her eyes soft.

"Will Anna be able to finish grade seven with us?"

Miss Alexander shifts the papers on her desk. "I don't know about that yet. I understand the funeral is at four o'clock next Tuesday at St. Joseph's. I intend to go."

"I'd like to go too."

"Do you think your parents could drive you out to Anna's place? I'd like to put together a package of school books for her," Miss Alexander says.

"I'm sure my dad would. I'll go too. Mom can't drive." I don't mention that she wouldn't want to go anyway. She didn't know Anna's mother and she doesn't like Mr. Lozowski.

oooooo

AT SUPPER, MOM says, "It's a shame for those kids. Six of them now with the baby. And Anna doing all the work. That father of hers is probably in town right now drowning his sorrows in the beer parlour."

I wish Mom wouldn't talk like that. I need to think about how things have changed so quickly. Poor Anna. Her mother is dead, and she won't be able to come to school. And poor me. I won't have my best friend in school.

Dad agrees to drive out to Anna's farm on Saturday.

"I'll come with you," I say.

Mom butts in. "I don't think that's a good idea. Your father will drop off the things for Anna. If you were there, you'd want to stay. I don't feel right about you spending time on that farm."

"I have to go, Mom."

I turn to my father. "Dad? I *need* to see Anna."

"Your mother and I will talk about it. Good night, Mags."

I go to bed determined to see Anna tomorrow. I'll throw myself under the car wheels if I have to.

oooooo

I'M SURPRISED THE next day when Mom says I can go. I guess Dad talked her into it. Mom has things for us to take to the family. She's made a gingerbread cake, and she takes a yellow baby blanket from her gift drawer.

"I crocheted this last winter. At least the child will be warm." Mom hands me some coloured wrapping paper.

I'm struggling to wrap the blanket when Mom says, "That parcel looks a mess. Let me straighten it."

I bite my tongue. I can't do anything right.

Dad and I drive in the big police car south out of town toward the line of hills on the horizon. Dad says it's seven miles on the dirt road to the four sections where the Lozowskis run their cattle.

I'm nervous about seeing Anna. I don't know if she'll be too upset to talk to me. Or what I should say about her mother. Or if I'll start to cry as soon as I see her. I grip the cake pan tightly the whole drive out.

We turn off at the corner just before the park grounds and drive along a small creek lined with trees. Dad parks the car close to the two-storey wooden house, and a little girl in bare feet with tight curly hair comes running out to meet us.

"You must be Helen," I say, smiling at her. She looks at me with a serious face and nods, then runs to the back door. Joe and Berny are bending over an old truck in the yard and wave to us.

Mr. Lozowski comes out the door, rubbing his unshaven cheeks and brushing back his dark hair. He's wearing dirty grey trousers with black suspenders. He nods at us. Anna comes out behind him, with a smaller girl hanging onto her skirt.

Anna sees me and runs to give me a tight hug.

"This is Lucy," Anna says, pushing the small girl forward. "Lucy, can you say hello to Maggie and her father?"

Lucy stares at us with big brown eyes. "Uh-hum." She reaches to Helen to be picked up.

Helen is very pretty, even with her dark hair in tangles. She isn't much bigger than Lucy, and she struggles to hold her younger sister in her arms.

Dad and Mr. Lozowski walk into the yard. Anna leads me inside.

I put the cake tin and the parcel on the kitchen table beside the dirty plates. The little girls come over and stare at the tin.

"Are you Anna's friend?" Helen asks.

"I'm her best friend," I tell her. "And I hear you're the girl with all the questions!"

Anna gives me a smile. Her eyes look tired. She goes to a wooden cradle and picks up the baby, kisses her, and hands her to me.

The baby is as light as a doll, but much warmer and softer than any doll I've ever had. Her pink face is all scrunched up. She whimpers a bit and kicks her thin legs loose from the blanket.

"We named her Isabella, after Mama," Anna says. "Bella for short."

"That's a beautiful name." I tighten the blanket around the baby and sit at the kitchen table, watching while Anna wedges wood into the stove and slides over a pan of milk.

Berny comes in the door. I see him at school, and he seems popular with the other grade four boys. Joe comes in too. Tall and good-looking, Joe's in grade ten and has the start of a beard on his chin. I hear he's smart, like Anna.

The boys nod at me, and Berny's eyes fix on the cake. "Can we have some?" he asks.

Anna says, "Okay, everyone can have a piece." She passes me a bottle to feed the baby.

It surprises me how quickly Bella starts sucking, her pink mouth gripping tightly to get the milk. I run my hand over the dark fuzz on her head and stroke her little hand. Her fingers close around mine and my heart gives a leap. She knows I'm here.

The two girls and Joe and Berny stand around munching the cake that Anna's cut. She offers me a piece, but I shake my head and tell her to have one herself.

I stroke Bella's warm head. "You *are* hungry, aren't you, little one?" I say. The baby stares solemnly up at me with big dark eyes, then stops sucking, and the tip of a pink tongue pushes out between her lips. Then she goes back to sucking. She smells of milk and something sweet like honey.

Anna smiles down at Bella. "She's a good baby. She loves her bottle, but it's hard at night because she wakes up every two hours."

"She's only a few days old. When will she sleep through the night?"

"Lucy didn't sleep all night until she was almost a year. Bella came early and she's small. I don't know when I'll get a decent sleep."

Anna knows more about babies than I ever will. There are smoky circles around her eyes. She's pale, but all her brothers and sisters have pale skin and dark hair like hers. The baby, too.

The kids are clustered around the table.

"Run away and play," Anna says. "Maggie and I are going to put Bella to sleep."

"I'll watch the girls," Berny says. He picks Lucy up and leads Helen out the door. The screen door bangs, slap, slap, as they leave.

Up the narrow stairs, Anna shows me where the boys share a room. Across the narrow hall is a room where Lucy and Helen share a bed. Bella sleeps with Anna in another room. None of the beds are made, and the tin pail by the door of Anna's room smells of dirty diapers.

Bella whimpers a bit while Anna changes her thin cloth diaper. I smile at Bella's tummy bulging out like a soft little hill. Expertly, Anna wraps Bella in the yellow blanket Mom made. With just her head peering out, the baby looks like she's inside a parcel.

"The blanket's beautiful," Anna says.

I sit on the bed and watch her pace back and forth, jiggling Bella in her arms until she falls asleep. Anna puts her down on the bed, and I bend over and touch her small hand. It curls around my finger again, as though she knows me, even in her sleep. Her ten tiny nails are like pearly drops of water.

I give Anna the school books with the note from Miss Alexander.

"I won't have time to do school work," Anna says, sliding them under the bed without reading the note.

"How long will you have to stay home to look after the baby?" I ask.

Anna's eyes start to fill with tears. "Until Bella grows up . . . I guess."

I move closer and touch her arm. "I'm so sorry about your mother. Can you tell me what happened?"

Anna

SATURDAY, APRIL 17

WE SIT ON the bed, and I take a breath. “Papa didn’t have time to go for the midwife because the baby came so quickly. She was already born when he woke up. Mama asked me to take care of the baby. I promised her I would.”

Maggie’s eyes are big.

“I was sitting right there beside Mama and I didn’t even know she was dead. I thought she was asleep.”

“Oh, Anna.” Maggie clutches my hand.

We look down at Bella lying on the bed. Her blue-veined eyelids quiver in her sleep. Every now and then her small lips tremble.

“Then Papa said he couldn’t manage six kids. I realized I’d have to be the mother in the family.”

I have never seen anyone’s eyes fill up with tears the way Maggie’s do now. They spill onto her cheeks like rain splashing off a roof.

I start to cry too. I can't help it. I haven't cried since that morning, but now I can't stop.

We're both crying, and I put my arms around Maggie. Her glasses have slipped down her nose and her tears are soaking my shoulder. When we finally stop, I feel exhausted, but not so alone.

I sit back and take a deep breath. "I feel so guilty, Maggie. I was with Mama when she died. I know I should have done something." I stop to take another breath. "I didn't think she'd die. I thought she'd get a good rest and then be up again. Like she was with the other kids."

"You couldn't have known, Anna."

"I'll never forget sitting there with my mother, not realizing she was dead."

I can feel myself shaking, and I realize it's cold inside the house. Just then I hear the squealing of brakes. Through the bedroom window I see Papa's truck fishtailing out of the yard. He probably lost his temper with Maggie's dad. Not a smart thing to do with an RCMP officer.

Maggie is wiping her eyes and doesn't hear the truck. I'm glad. I sit back on the bed, and we stay there for a time, holding hands.

"I've got so much to do here, Maggie. Bella needs bottles night and day. I have to make breakfast and lunches and get the boys off to school. I'm the one who has to do the washing. There are so many diapers because Lucy's still wearing them. The washer is in the shed at the back of the house and all the hot water has to be carried from the stove. Papa's mostly out in the fields because some cows are still calving. He doesn't always come home at night to help me make supper and put the little ones to bed."

"It sounds like too much, Anna," Maggie says.

She'll never understand that this is my life now. Her life is so easy. Just homework and time to read. Time to be by herself. Her parents take care of everything else.

I hear someone on the stairs. It's Lucy crawling up on her hands and knees. I pick her up and kiss her fat cheek. She sucks her thumb and leans into me.

"This one's still a baby. She shouldn't be on the stairs by herself, but I can't always watch her."

Maggie's father is calling and we say goodbye. We're both worn out.

Maggie

SUNDAY, APRIL 18,

AND MONDAY, APRIL 19

I SLEEP RESTLESSLY all night, tossing around on the chesterfield. It's still dark when I wake up, and I've wrapped my arms around the pillow, the way I wrapped them around Bella. I guess I dozed off, because there's a pale light in the sky when I wake up to the shrill sound of a siren.

An ambulance has stopped at the side door of the barracks. The flaring light on the roof sends yellow circles across the yard. I jump out of bed in time to see two men hurry into the basement. They carry a stretcher to the side door, and a few minutes later they come out with a man lying on it. They slam the door of the ambulance and drive away.

Mom's wearing her dressing gown when she comes into the room.

"Away from that window," she says to me.

"Who is it?" I ask.

"The prisoner tried to kill himself. Dad says he'll survive and they're taking him to the hospital in Regina. When he gets out, he'll go into a bigger prison there. Now get back into bed."

Her voice is sharp. It feels as though I've done something wrong.

After Mom goes out, Tommy pads into my room in his bare feet.

"That was the murderer, you know," I say.

"I heard Mommy." He squirms with excitement. "I bet the guy hid the fork from his dinner tray under his mattress. Then in the middle of the night he stabbed himself in the heart twenty times!"

I am disgusted and roll over with my back to him.

"Bet I'm right," he says as he pads back to his own room.

I have a sick feeling in my stomach about the prisoner. The poor man.

Later, Mom calls me to come into the kitchen. "Take the breakfast tray to your grandmother, please."

As I reach to pick up the tray, Mom says, "I notice you never complain when you're asked to do anything for her."

I turn away. "You're right. I don't."

Gram drinks the tea and eats a bit of toast while I tell her about the prisoner. "It's heartbreaking," Gram says. "There are things in this world we have a hard time understanding."

"I need to tell you something else that's hard to understand. My friend Anna's mother died having a baby last week. Anna promised her mother she'd take care of the baby. And she has to cook and clean for everybody in the family."

"That poor girl," Gram says softly. She shifts in the bed and shakes her head. "It's not right to expect Anna to carry that load. Is there no one else to help?"

"I don't think so," I say. "Her dad has to work around the farm and he's in town all the time. A woman called Mrs. Covey lives close by, but she has children of her own. Anna knows it's up to her."

"That will be hard for a girl of her age," Gram says.

"Well, she's promised, and I know Anna, Gram. If she makes a promise, she'll keep it. She's like that."

Gram gives me a hug. "You care about Anna, don't you?"

"I do," I say.

My grandmother truly understands me.

Gram says she plans to rest in bed all day. She likes to look out into the treetops. I like it too. When the sun filters into the room through the branches, my bedroom becomes a shady veranda. For the last few days, Gram hasn't pinned her white hair in a swirl but has let lie it loose on the pillow. It makes her look like an angel.

I hate to say goodbye when I leave for school.

It's lonely without Anna in the class. In the afternoon, Carolyn gives out invitations to her birthday party next Saturday.

Carolyn always wears a bow in her hair. Today it's yellow. She has a smug look on her face and what looks like a dandelion on her head.

"Coming to my party?" she asks as we go out the school door at the end of the day.

What can I say? All the other girls will be going, but I don't want to. "Not sure," I say as I keep walking.

Carolyn says, "You're mad at me because I didn't invite your best friend, aren't you?"

I don't say anything. Anna's not in school these days. Even if she was invited, she couldn't get into town on a Saturday.

Carolyn hurries along behind me. "I hear she's stuck out on the farm looking after the baby."

"I've seen the baby," I tell her. "She's adorable."

"You've been out to Anna's farm?"

"My dad took me on the weekend, and I got to feed the baby. By the way, Anna wouldn't come to your party. She has responsibilities now. She doesn't have time for parties."

I turn toward the barracks hill. "I might have to be with my grandmother on Saturday. I'll let you know."

Carolyn turns down her street without saying another word, her chin leading the way.

When I get home, Mom says Gram is sleeping and tells me not to go into her room. Tommy and I sit at the kitchen table eating cookies.

"Wanna hear my new joke, Maggie?" he says.

"No, I don't."

"I'll tell you 'cause it's short." He's spraying cookie crumbs out of his mouth. "Why does an elephant wear red nail polish?"

"I don't know and I don't care."

"I'll tell you anyway," he bursts out. "An elephant wears red nail polish so he can hide in a cherry tree!"

His snickering is *too* much.

"Scram," I say.

"That's no way to talk to your brother," Mom says. "And, Maggie, when you go in to see Gram, please don't sit on the bed. Your grandmother's having trouble getting comfortable."

I'd noticed that too. I tiptoe into the bedroom to see if Gram's awake. She is, and I pull up a chair beside her.

I show Gram the scarf I've finished making. "I don't know what I was thinking. Who needs a wool scarf in May? Maybe one with holes would be perfect for a hot day!"

I count on my grandmother to laugh at my joke, and she does.

I put my head down beside her on the bed and she runs her fingers slowly through my hair. It makes my head feel heavy and dreamy. Only one person in the world can make me feel like that.

∘∘∘∘∘∘∘

GRAM'S NOT HUNGRY, but she has a few spoonfuls of soup for supper. Later we decide I'll read *Thumbelina* to her. We both love the story of little girl who floats down the stream in a walnut shell boat.

"Your voice is very expressive, Maggie," Gram says. "You could read to Tommy sometime."

"I'd rather read to you."

Gram falls asleep before I finish the story. I leave quietly so I don't wake her.

Dad's in his armchair reading some reports. Even though I'm too big, I plunk myself down on his lap. "Dad, how did the prisoner try to kill himself?"

Dad shifts the papers so I'm not sitting on them. "That's police business, Mags. Don't worry your head about it."

"But, Dad, he must have felt terrible about murdering his wife and his baby. So terrible he tried to kill himself."

I'd be in big trouble if I told Dad I'd gone to the cells and heard the man crying.

Dad lifts me off his lap. "The man's probably mentally ill," he says. "Off you go now, Mags."

I lie in bed and realize I don't know anything about mental illness. I wonder if it means your mind is confused and you can feel two different things at the same time. I couldn't be like that. To me, a thing is either right or wrong.

Anna

THURSDAY, APRIL 22

TONIGHT IS NOT a good night. Nothing seems right for poor Bella. Her face is red from screaming and she's breathing too fast. A real mother would know what to do.

I don't understand why Mama had to die. You have to expect your parents will die when they're old, but Mama was only thirty-six. She told me she and Papa were in love and so happy to come to Canada. They had Joe right away, then the rest of us one after another.

I sometimes think of Mama like the painting of the Madonna and child in the chapel at church. The Madonna looks down in such a loving the way at the baby in her arms. We had love like that from Mama.

But what do you do when that love is gone? You're lonely and your skin feels cold all the time.

I'm not strong like Mama, but I love Bella and all my family as much as she did. They need to be cared for and loved. I can do it. I *will* do it. I like to think that Mama is somewhere nearby watching me.

I rock Bella in my arms for hours tonight. This old house creaks in the wind, and my back is cold. In the middle of the night, I take her to the kitchen to heat up milk. I light the lamp and walk around the house.

This is my life. The beaten-up brown couch and the old armchair with the stuffing leaking out the back. The faded red carpet. The kitchen floor filthy because the kids spill food and I don't have the time or energy to wash it.

About four o'clock, Boo wakes up and mews around my legs. I settle into the armchair, holding both the cat and Bella. His warm fur and beating heart seem to calm Bella. I stroke the cat and kiss my sister's face. Out the window I watch the sky lighten from black to grey. The morning birds begin their chatter and there is a crescent of yellow in the sky toward the eastern fields. The sun is coming up on this sad day for us.

Mama's funeral is this afternoon, and I want to make sure our family looks good. I clean up the girls and take my time brushing their hair. Helen squeals and ducks away from me when I try to get the tangles out of her hair. The girls' dresses are clean, though they're not ironed.

I decide to wear Mama's best blouse with the lace collar. I take the white blouse from the drawer in my parents' dresser. It's cool and silky on my arms and has the spicy smell of Mama's skin. I look at myself in the mirror. The blouse is too big for me and falls loosely over my shoulders. I would never look right in Mama's blouse, but I need it today for courage.

I straighten my shoulders and do my hair in fresh braids, then pick up Bella and come down to join the boys and Papa who are waiting at the front door.

Papa has put on the white shirt he wears to sell cattle and his hair is slicked back over his forehead. He looks at the blouse but doesn't say anything. The boys are stiff and nervous in their white shirts.

"You all look good. Mama would be proud of us," I say.

The boys pile into the back of the truck and the girls ride with me in the cab. Papa takes a drink out of the bottle on the seat between us. No one says a word on the trip into town. Bella falls asleep before we reach the church.

The casket is on a stand near the altar, covered with a white cloth. Our family is shown to the front pew, with Papa, rigid and silent, sitting closest to the casket. I sit beside him, Bella asleep with her head against my shoulder. Helen and Lucy sit beside me next to the boys, who look scared.

I stare at the casket. Mama's cold body is inside, so close to us. I have to push that thought out of my mind. I won't think of it.

I remember Mama that last night with her eyes closed and her hands crossed on her chest. How can someone as real as my mother be put in the earth? I can't let myself think about that. I want to remember the time we sat with her warm arms around me. "You are my strong one," she told me.

The priest goes on and on, talking in Latin. Helen and Lucy are restless beside me. The priest sprinkles holy water on the casket and waves incense in the air. Something wakes Bella and she starts to cry. She cries good and loud, as only Bella can.

Papa jumps up and snatches her out of my arms. He's muttering under his breath as he stomps down the aisle with his head down. I turn and see everyone staring at him. The pounding of his boots echoes through the startled silence, followed by the bang of the outside door. I think I catch sight of Maggie in the back row.

Papa has left us alone in the church. We're his children. He's not here with us for his own wife's funeral. How could he be so selfish? I put my arms around Helen and Lucy and pull them close.

Outside, after the service, Papa hands Bella back to me. She's still crying. He looks sheepish as he shakes hands with a few people who've come to the service. Mr. and Mrs. Covey have come, and Miss Alexander too. That's wonderful of her, and she gives me such a warm smile as she walks over to me.

"Your mother would be proud of you, Anna. I'll bring out more school books so you can keep up your grade seven work. We can work together so you get credit for the year."

I'm worried that she'll get too close to Papa and smell liquor. "I'll try, Miss Alexander." I turn my attention to Bella, trying to settle her.

Papa's made a bad impression. I can tell by the looks people give him. I'm ashamed for Mama's sake. People will feel sorry for us.

There's no sign of Maggie, and I hope she wasn't there to see the way my father behaved. I don't care so much about the others, but I want Maggie to think well of our family.

Maggie

SATURDAY, APRIL 24,
TO MONDAY, APRIL 26

IT'S SATURDAY MORNING, and I bring breakfast to Gram in bed. She doesn't touch anything but the tea. She sleeps all morning, and I decide I might as well go to Carolyn's party. There's no chance to tell Gram I'm going.

Like everyone else, I'm wearing my best dress and carrying a present when I arrive at the door of the big white house on Aspen. There's a purple bow in the birthday girl's hair today. The first thing she does is lead us into her bedroom to admire the horse posters on the wall. There's a framed picture of her horse, Chester, on the dresser.

Anna rides horses on her farm, but she doesn't act so horsey.

"Mommy and Daddy gave me a new saddle for my birthday. I can't show you because it's at the stable," Carolyn says.

Then we have to admire the orange-and-white striped canopy festooned over her bed.

If I had a big room like this, I'd have lots of bookshelves and a table by the window where I could leave my pencil crayons out and not have to tidy them up every time Mom sets the kitchen table. And I would never in a million years sleep under an orange-and-white circus tent!

We play a childish game where you pass around a present that's been wrapped in layers of paper. When Carolyn's mom says STOP, you take off one layer of paper and then keep repeating the whole thing until the last person gets to open the present. It turns out to be a pair of ankle socks with horseshoes on them.

Then we have sandwiches and sing "Happy Birthday" around an angel food cake with pink icing. Carolyn's mother wraps a piece in waxed paper for me to take home for Tommy. I plan to give it to Gram.

oooooo

I RUSH UP the stairs and along the hall to the bedroom to tell Gram about the party. I'm stunned to see the bed empty. It's completely bare. The sheets have been stripped off. It's just the blue mattress and two pillows without covers.

"Where's Gram?" I yell, tearing back down the hall to my father, who is sitting in his shirt sleeves at the kitchen table.

"Come here, Mags." He lifts me onto his lap.

The whole place is quiet.

"Where's Gram?" I ask again.

Dad wraps his long arms around me and pulls my head tight against him. His voice is close to my ear. "Gram's gone to Heaven. She's gone to be with Gramps."

"What do you mean?"

"Gram had cancer. There was nothing the doctors could do."

I knew it. I knew my grandmother was sick. My eyes start to hurt. "She was fine when I left for the birthday party."

And then I know she wasn't fine. She stayed in bed too much. But I never thought she'd die. Tears are gushing out of me like a newly struck well.

"I didn't say goodbye," I hear myself wailing. "I was going to tell her about the party." I'm still holding the squished cake.

Dad takes the cake and puts it on the table. He holds me while I cry.

When the storm of tears finally lets up, I put my head on Dad's chest and curl up inside his strong arms. Just like I did when I was little.

I raise my head and look at him. "She was your mother, Dad. You must be upset."

"I loved her," he says. "She was a wonderful person."

Would I say that about my mother?

I sit up. "Where *is* Mom? Where's Tommy?"

"Tommy's with his friend up the street. Your mother's talking to the minister. I wanted to be here when you came home." Dad gives me his handkerchief to blow my nose.

"I was going to stay with Gram in the summer holidays."

"I'm so sorry, little Mags."

oooooo

THAT NIGHT THERE are clean sheets on my bed. Mom says, "It's okay for you to sleep here, Maggie."

At first it makes me feel funny lying in the bed where my grandmother died, but I lay my cheek on the pillow where Gram's white hair was spread out and remember how she looked like an angel. I pray with all my heart that Gram is happy in Heaven with Gramps. Her hair is swirled up with the silver pin, and Gramps is beside her, wearing his old straw hat.

I can't fall asleep, so I get out of bed and stand by the window looking out at the empty black night. I try to take in the enormous fact that my grandmother has gone from this earth. A person so special to me is dead. I stand until my legs grow weak, then crawl back under the covers.

oooooo

MOM WAKES ME on Monday, but it's hard to get moving and I'm almost late for school. At recess, I stay in the room to talk to Miss Alexander. I stand behind her where she's writing on the blackboard. The minute she turns to look at me I start to cry. I'm embarrassed to be bawling like a kindergarten kid.

The words sputter out. "I didn't even say goodbye... or tell Gram how much I loved her. I got back from Carolyn's party... and the bed was empty. How could she die so quickly?"

Miss Alexander leans over and puts her arms around me. I push my face into her soft blouse and cry. When I can't cry any more, she walks me back to my desk and sits down across from me. She takes both my hands in hers.

"You've told me how much you loved your grandmother," she says softly. "She knew that."

I hope Gram knew my heart was filled with love for her.

We sit like that for a while, and Miss Alexander tells me she plans to visit Anna on the farm. "I'll make a pie for the family."

"When Dad took me to see Anna she let me feed the baby. They're calling her Bella."

"What a lovely name. *Bella* means 'beautiful' in Spanish."

I wonder if Anna knows that. "The baby *is* beautiful."

I'm still at my desk when the class comes back. I keep my head down so no one will know I've been crying. It's all been too much. First Anna's mother dies, then Anna can't come to school, and now my own grandmother has died. Nothing will ever be right again.

No one talks to me all afternoon. Not even Jerry.

At home, Mom says, "You'd better get to the piano practice you missed this morning."

"As if I care. I hate piano." I put my books down on the table.

"Stop that talk. And get your books off the kitchen table."

I pick up the books and march into my room where I can be by myself. Where I can remember my grandmother, who would never, ever be mean to me.

Anna

SUNDAY, APRIL 25

AS USUAL ON a weekend, the boys are out riding with Papa. I've loved horses from the first time Papa taught us all to ride, but I never have time to ride now.

Bella's asleep at last up on my bed. She's safe there because she's still too little to roll off. When I'm in the kitchen, she sleeps in the cradle Dad made for all of us. I had to remind Joe again this morning to milk Dover. Dad never makes him help around the house. "Girls' work," Joe says. I have the feeling he can hardly wait to get out on his own.

The girls are standing around the kitchen table, trying to help me make bread. Lucy's on her tiptoes to see over the edge of the table. Lucy and Helen each have a ball of dough. They copy me as I knead the dough, the heels of their little hands pushing through the soft dough. Every now and then they break off a piece and eat it.

I hear car tires crunching on the driveway and look out the window to see Miss Alexander's car. It's the blue Dodge I've seen her drive after school. I'm torn between embarrassment that she'll see the shabby place we live in and the thrill of seeing her. Imagine coming all the way out here to see us on a Sunday. Imagine a single woman owning a car!

Quickly, I put the dough back in the mixing bowl and pull the pieces out of the girls' sticky hands. I send them off to the wash basin and give my own hands a quick wash. I open the door as Miss Alexander walks up the path, balancing a school bag and a big tin in her arms.

"Hello, Miss Alexander," I say, feeling shy as I walk to meet her.

"How are you, Anna?"

I look a mess. I'm wearing Mom's old apron, and it's covered in flour. "Not too bad."

I invite her into the kitchen and introduce the girls. "Meet Helen and Lucy, my little sisters." I wonder what she thinks of their faded dresses and their hair not brushed. "The baby's asleep upstairs."

Miss Alexander puts the tin on the table and kneels in front of the girls. She gives each of them a kiss on the cheek, and then stands and holds out her arms to hug me. Her hair smells of roses. I could bury myself in it, but I pull back and try to brush the flour off my apron.

"I'm sure you're tired, Anna," Miss Alexander says.

I don't say anything.

"Of course you are, you poor girl. What a responsibility you've got here."

The boys come crashing into the kitchen, followed by Papa. Miss Alexander knows the boys from school. She sometimes gives Berny special help with his reading.

"I brought you something," she says, taking a big pie out of the tin.

"Homemade pie!" Joe says.

"What kind?" asks Berny.

"Raisin," Miss Alexander says.

Berny's grinning. "My favourite."

Papa goes over to shake her hand. "Very kind of you, Miss Alexander."

"Can we eat it now?" Helen asks.

Miss Alexander looks at me. "Why not?"

Lucy edges closer. "Um-hum."

"That's what Lucy says," Helen explains to Miss Alexander.

Papa gets a knife and cuts the pie. Dark, fat raisins topple onto the plates as he serves us each a piece. My family take big forkfuls of pie, as though they haven't seen anything like it for months. Well, in fact, they haven't. Mama certainly didn't bake when she was so big with the baby and I never learned to make a pie. I ask Miss Alexander if she'd like to come upstairs and see Bella.

Her blue skirt brushes the steep stairs as she goes ahead of me into the bedroom. We stand beside the bed looking at Bella, who's asleep flat on her back. She's kicked off the covers and her little arms and legs are splayed out on both sides.

"She's a beautiful baby," Miss Alexander says in a quiet voice. "I hope she's sleeping through a few hours in the night."

I look at the way Miss Alexander's hair curls over her shoulders. Everything about her is just right. I don't want to tell her what last night was like.

"Not too bad."

I catch a look at myself in the mirror. I didn't have time to brush my own hair this morning. There's dried bread dough stuck to one arm.

"Let's leave Bella to sleep as long as she can," Miss Alexander whispers. "Let me show you the school work I've brought for you."

The boys have cleared out, leaving the kitchen table a mess. The two girls are still in their chairs, Lucy's pudgy legs swinging in the air as she pushes the last of the pie into her mouth with her fingers.

Miss Alexander hands me the bag she's brought. It's heavy with books and papers, and I look at them in despair. "I'll try, Miss Alexander, but I don't have much time in the day."

She's brought the math textbook from my desk and some grammar sheets, which she knows I do well. I can't imagine how I'll find any time, day or night.

She hands me a book. "This is from my own collection," she says. "It's *Anne of Avonlea*. I've always loved the *Anne* books, and in this one Anne becomes a teacher."

"I'll love it, Miss Alexander." I look at the picture of a grown-up Anne on the cover.

"I thought it would be just the book for you. She's the Anne with the 'e' and you're the Anna with the 'a.'"

How perfect.

Bella start to whimper upstairs, and I leave Miss Alexander wiping the faces of the two girls. I take a minute to tidy my braids and take off the apron.

When I come downstairs carrying Bella, Lucy is on Miss Alexander's lap. Helen stands leaning into Miss Alexander's knees while she plays a singing finger game with them.

Here's the church and here's the steeple.
Look inside and here are the people!

They giggle and try it with their own fingers while I get milk from the ice box and put it on the stove to heat.

"Could I give Bella her bottle?" Miss Alexander asks. I pass Bella to her and the baby settles right down in Miss Alexander's arms. She knows exactly how to give a baby a bottle. She talks to the girls as Bella sucks at her bottle. While they're occupied, I take the dough from the bowl and give it a last kneading before shaping it into four loaves. That will have to last the week.

"Would you like to have a walk down by the creek?" I ask Miss Alexander.

"I'd love that," she says. She shifts Bella onto her shoulder to burp her.

"First I have to put Lucy on the potty," I say.

We both smile at Lucy, her little pink bottom wiggling in excitement.

"You finished?" I ask, and she nods and runs to get her sweater. Bella is wrapped in a blanket when I pass her to Miss Alexander. We head out toward the creek.

The air smells of damp earth and fresh spring beginnings. The little girls scamper around, then the boys come along and join us. They're excited to have a visitor, especially a teacher.

Miss Alexander smiles at Joe. "You've grown taller this year." Berny catches up to walk along beside her, and she asks, "How's your reading coming along, Berny?"

"A little better," he answers, grinning up at her.

The warm days have started little green shoots along the side of the path. "Don't step on them," I tell the girls. "They'll be shooting stars soon."

"I know shooting stars," Miss Alexander says. "Such delicate spring flowers."

"Mama loved them," I tell her.

The creek is full after the winter rains and small patches of snow still shelter under the trees. When the girls run on ahead with the boys, Miss Alexander and I have a quiet moment to ourselves.

She pauses and looks at me. "I have something to tell you, Anna. It's about Maggie. I'm sorry to tell you that her grandmother has died."

"Oh, no," I say.

Miss Alexander puts her arm around me. "You and I both know how much Maggie loved her grandmother."

I lean into Miss Alexander. "I feel terrible for her."

It's seems strange that Maggie's grandmother and my mother should die so close to the same time.

I hate to see Miss Alexander leave. I stand with the girls, still feeling the warmth of her goodbye hug. We wave as we watch the blue car get smaller and then disappear as it turns onto the main road.

I wonder when I'll be able to see Maggie to tell her how sorry I am.

Maggie

SATURDAY, MAY 1,
AND SUNDAY, MAY 2

IT'S HOT OUTSIDE, but our church is cool and smells of stale air. Mrs. Olafson is playing a gloomy piece on the organ and most people are already seated. They talk in hushed voices the way people do in church. Coloured light falls from the tall arched windows onto my grandmother's coffin, which is draped in a purple cloth.

We take our seats in the front row. I sit beside Dad and hold his hand. Tommy climbs on Mom's lap. We're close enough to smell the sickly-sweet white carnations in the vase beside the coffin.

I turn around and see lots of people, including Jerry and his mother, and Miss Alexander. Toward the back, Otto sits beside May from the office.

All week I've been remembering the afternoon Gram died. What kind of a girl would be passing around a stupid pair of horseshoe socks and eating cake when her grandmother is dying? Why didn't anyone tell me she was dying? Why didn't I figure it out myself?

The minister announces a hymn and everyone stands to sing. For the first time, the words of a hymn mean something to me.

My own dear land, where'er my footsteps wander,
... No dearer land to me in all the earth.

And the memory comes of walking across a field with Gram to take lunch to Gramps. I'm holding Gram's hand and swinging the tin lunch pail. Gram stops to smell the wild roses and shows me how the leaves on rose bushes have the same delicate smell as the flowers. That's exactly the kind of thing she'd notice.

But she's gone. I'll never melt against her when she hugs me. Never hear her laugh when I say something funny. I want to go back to those days.

The minister stands at the front of the church. He's tall and thin but his voice is deep. "Mrs. Neilson was a hardworking farmer's wife. A woman who had a deep love for her family."

Gram loved me. And I can never forgive myself for not being there to tell her I loved her back.

The minister says, "I'd like to offer comfort to the family by reminding them that suffering the loss of a beloved family member can bring with it a new and unexpected blessing of an equally deep capacity for joy."

I listen carefully.

"Look to your lives. I encourage you to open your hearts. You will be deepened and widened by this experience. And through your loss and grief, you will find your life richer."

I don't understand what he's saying because of the hurt space inside my chest that gets squeezed with every breath I take. I try to say the words of the psalm we're singing, "I will lift up my eyes unto the hills," but I get no further than the first line because I have the sudden sharp memory of Gramps pointing to the line of rolling blue hills west of the farm.

Now both my grandparents are dead. My knees are wobbly when the minister tells us to stand and sing.

Blest be the tie that binds . . .
When for a while we part,
This thought will soothe our pain
That we shall still be joined in heart
And one day meet again.

To be joined in heart forever to Gram. If I believe it, then maybe I'll be able to say goodbye.

When the service is over, I stand beside my parents as people come and speak to us. Miss Alexander kisses my cheek. Jerry gives me an embarrassed look and smiles shyly. His mother takes my hands in both of hers and says, "I know how much you'll miss your grandmother, Maggie."

I can't think of what I should say. A funny sound comes out of my throat and Dad squeezes my arm. Mom looks steadily ahead. She doesn't usually show how she feels. If she was my real mother, she'd be more like me and show every feeling she has.

Behind the church, four men lower my grandmother's coffin into a hole in the ground. The minister says a prayer, but I don't hear it. Inside my head I'm saying, *Goodbye, Gram. Goodbye.* My legs feel so heavy, I don't think I can keep standing.

Then it's over. Our family walks the five blocks home. Mom hurries on ahead to get tea ready to serve the people who'll be coming over.

Mom uses her best cups and saucers, which are almost never out of the china cabinet. A lace cloth is on the dining room table along with plates of sandwiches and cake. Lots of people come to the house, and I'm told to pass things around. Tommy stuffs himself on butter tarts, but I don't feel like eating.

oooooo

WHEN I'M IN bed, I think about the funeral for Anna's mother just last week. I'm glad I slipped into the back row of the church and hurried out at the end. I don't think Anna saw me, but I saw her. Her face was pale, as white as the blouse she was wearing. I'll never tell her I know her dad stomped out of the service with poor Bella screaming so hard. Would people have gone to the Lozowski farm to drink tea afterward? Somehow I don't think so.

Mom goes into Tommy's bedroom and I hear him say, "Will we ever see Gram again?" Mom says something that I can't hear.

She comes into my room and sits on the edge of the bed. "You'll be lonely without your Gram, won't you, Maggie?"

"I will, Mom."

"We'll all have to keep going." I feel her lips on my cheek and then she goes out. It's not until afterwards that I realize I could have said I was glad I still had her. I could have said it, but I didn't.

I wake in the dark to the sound of crying, but it's just the bare tree branches brushing against my window.

oooooo

IT'S SUNDAY, AND the rain outside makes a dreary day that matches my mood. We all went to church, but since we've come back, Dad has gone down to the office, Tommy is playing in his room, and Mom is cleaning again.

I don't know why, but I feel anger rising up in me in a flood. "Haven't you heard of a day of rest, Mom?"

Mom turns off the vacuum. "What did you say?"

I hesitate but plunge in anyway. "Ever heard of a day of rest? You're always cleaning."

"I'm cleaning, dear girl, because the house is dirty after all those people were here yesterday. And you don't help hanging around in my way. Tommy's got enough sense to play in his room."

Her scrawny arms hold the vacuum hose like a weapon.

"Take a break, Mom. You can clean tomorrow. That is, if you don't have anything more interesting to do."

"What on earth do you mean by that?" Mom is angry now. Her tight lips show it. It feels as though my nerves are wound up. I can't stop.

"Other mothers are busy doing interesting things. Jerry's mom teaches Sunday School and works with the youth group. Carolyn's mother works part-time at the stables. Even Miss Alexander who teaches all day coaches slow readers after school. You don't do anything but clean, clean, clean."

Mom says nothing.

I'm scared I've gone too far. Then she starts the vacuum cleaner again. "Out of my way."

The grinding noise gets inside my head and sets my nerves jangling. I'm stuck here with a person who doesn't understand one single thing about me.

I stomp out, yelling, "You're a very boring person. I'm glad you're not my real mother."

I'm out the door and down the stairs. I'm not sure if Mom heard me. I'd better stay out. I walk quickly along Birch Street toward town.

Couples stroll on the street and people sit on their verandas talking. Young kids pedal their tricycles along the sidewalks. I give Judy, a little neighbour girl, a push on her bike. She laughs as I help her zoom ahead and begs me to do it again.

Mrs. Davidson is across the street with her daughter. Shirley is nine and runs toward her mother. Mrs. Davidson picks her up and swings her around and around. They're laughing and holding hands as they walk away.

A man is crossing the road, wheeling himself in a wheelchair. One of his pant legs is folded up, which means there's absolutely nothing inside. I can't help staring. The man's not smiling, and I'm sure he's a veteran. The terrible war is over, but even in our small town we have reminders. It would be horrible to have only one leg. You could never ride a bike.

The purple lilac blossoms on First Avenue are almost open and their sweet smell already fills the air. I stick my nose into the heavy heads. "It's the smell of summer coming," Gram said when I was little. When I remember something she said, something as wonderful as that, it helps my brain to calm down.

As I turn onto Front Street, the freight train going east comes up the track, speeding through town. The engine's three headlights flare down the track, and the whistle shrills a message. *Quick! Jump on! Come away. Away.*

The sun is behind me, lower in the sky now. I've been walking a long time. Mom and Dad will be worried. I should go back. But I like being out here alone, seeing what I want to see, feeling what I want to feel.

The street lights come on. It must be later than I thought. By the time I turn up the hill to the barracks the sky is turning smoky grey. If Mom didn't hear what I said before I left, I might not be in too much trouble. I'll get it for being late, but not for being rude.

I walk down the hall into the living room, where Mom and Dad are reading the paper. They both look at me, and for a minute they don't say anything. Maybe they're not angry.

Then Dad says, "What are you doing staying out so late, Mags? You didn't tell us where you were going."

"I was fine, Dad. What's wrong with taking a stroll around town?"

"Mags, we know you're upset that your grandmother has died, and I'm sure you need time to think about it. But it's thoughtless of you not to consider that we might wonder where you were. Please don't go off like that without telling us again or you'll be in trouble."

"Sorry, Dad."

Mom's voice is sharp. "Your supper's in the oven. Eat, and then get right into bed. And I want you to clean up your own room next week. I hope you know how to use a vacuum."

"I'm sure I can figure it out."

Mom shakes her head. "Why are you getting so difficult?"

oooooo

I STAND BY the window in my pyjamas. If my parents think I'm a thoughtless and difficult person, then that's what I am. Maggie Neilson: thoughtless and difficult and proud of it! Temper like a spark, too.

Low in the sky to the west, I see the last of this day. Streaks of crimson and orange layer the horizon for a few glorious moments. Then suddenly all the brightness is gone and the whole world is dark. As I watch, magically in twos and threes and then in hundreds, stars appear out of deep space, filling the entire sky. My heart bursts with wonder. I am weak and insignificant on this earth, but I'm also part of this vast universe.

Is Gram somewhere up there? I like to believe that inside that vastness there might be a place called Heaven.

A place where everyone lives forever. Maybe there's a big farm kitchen up there. Gramps will be sitting in his favourite chair. Gram will be kneading a batch of bread on the wooden table. Maybe my real mother will be there with them, sitting at the table making conversation. Maybe there are angels, and Gram can say to one of them, "Pour us a cup of tea, will you?"

The truth is, I don't know where my real mother is and I don't know where Gram and Gramps are. But I know they're not here with me.

Anna

SUNDAY, MAY 9

IT'S MOTHER'S DAY, but nobody around me knows it. The girls are too little and the boys are too busy and Papa never figured out this special day. I long for Mama all day.

SUNDAY, MAY 9

I HATE MOTHER'S Day. Hate it.

I made a stupid card for Mom. Tommy gave her a teapot stand he made in kindergarten. It's made out of popsicle sticks glued together. Without a doubt, it's the ugliest thing ever created on this earth.

I'm glad I decided not to give her the scarf.

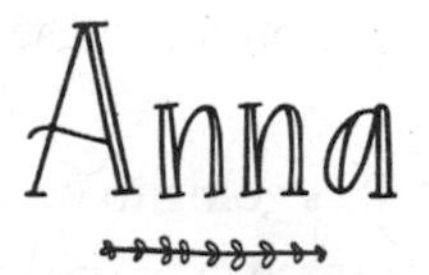

Anna

MONDAY, MAY 10

THE SUN CATCHES the red tail of the hawk as it circles lower and lower over the yard.

"Papa, there's a hawk by the barn!" I yell. He hears me and runs from the woodpile to see what the hawk's after. It's Boo!

Papa's yelling frightens the hawk, which flaps its powerful wings and soars away high over the south field. Papa comes back into the house carrying Boo, who isn't hurt but is trembling with fright.

"Boo got a bad scare," Papa says to the girls.

"You're okay, little puss. You're safe now," Helen says. She cradles her pet and kisses his black nose. Lucy wriggles to get down and stroke Boo, her small face wrinkled with concern.

Papa sits at the table, and I pass him a cup of coffee. He's been outside chopping wood in the stand of poplars behind the barn. Usually when he works to get a pile of firewood, it means he's going away.

"Come have a cup of coffee," he says to me. He forgets I don't like coffee.

"It's okay, Papa. Bella's going to wake up soon."

The girls are still fussing over the cat.

"Come on, girls. Put Boo down and finish your porridge." I go over and check the temperature of the water in the tub on the stove.

"Why do you heat water now?" Papa asks.

"To do the laundry, Papa! Lucy and Bella are both in diapers, don't you remember? I'm trying very hard to toilet train Lucy."

Papa has no idea what I do all day. Or what Mama did.

"I know there is much work, Anna." Papa reaches to take my hand. His hand is rough. A farmer's hands. There's dirt under his nails and in the cracks along his fingers. I pull my hand back.

I want to remind him how unfair it is that the boys go to school and I can't. But what's the point? I'd make him feel more guilty and nothing would change. The truth is, I couldn't go to school and still keep my promise to Mama. And I'm keeping my promise.

Papa rubs his grubby hands together. "Anna, I wish to get a woman to help you. You know there is no money to pay."

"I know that."

Papa pats my shoulder, then gets up and carries the tub of hot water to the washing shed behind the house. He comes back with the tub full of cold well water and puts it on the stove.

The girls dawdle over their porridge. "Eat up," I tell them.

From upstairs, Bella gives her special cry. A cry I know so well, the cry that means she's hungry. I go up to change her, then come back down to heat a bottle.

Papa's still at the table, helping Lucy finish her porridge. "I feed Bella today," he says.

That's a first.

I pass Bella to him, and he watches as she gulps her milk. She's such a tidy bundle in his big arms.

"Bella's almost four weeks old now," I say.

I notice when people hold Bella in their arms, even Papa, their eyes go soft and their face changes. It's as though their whole body softens, holding a baby.

Papa turns to me. "She looks like our Mama, you think?"

I think it every time I look at Bella. Right now I don't trust myself to say anything.

The girls stand close to Papa, watching him feed Bella, while I go out to the shed to do the laundry. Papa brings

Bella outside, and the girls follow while I hang the diapers on the line. I'm ashamed to see these old diapers out in the open. They're so worn, more grey than white.

We stand and look across the yard to the creek.

"Do you know," Papa says pointing to the trees along the creek bank, "your mama and I plant those trees together when we came from Poland in 1932?"

"Mama told me they were box elder trees."

"The farmer who sold to us said box elders, they stand strong in prairie winds. We do not know those winds then. The man promised they would grow quickly. Sixteen years. So tall now."

A breeze catches the new elder leaves. In the noon sun they swing and spin in shades of milky white and green.

"Mama and I mark this a special place. A place for our family to grow."

I'm surprised to hear Papa talking like this.

He has a faraway look in his eyes. "We were just married with big adventures to come. By ship across the Atlantic, then a long train ride to Deep Creek." Papa blinks his eyes and smiles at me. "We came for a better life. Canada is good to us."

Somehow, hearing Papa talk about these things, I don't mind the way he speaks. I understand how important it is for him to live here in Canada. To live on this land.

I understand how important his family is too. And now I must take Mama's place to help him.

"Have to work now, girls," Papa says. "I ride to the north field to round up cattle."

We go back into the kitchen, and he puts Bella in her cradle. She's content, her tummy full, grabbing at her feet with her hands.

I know what it means when Papa brings cattle into the pen near the barn. It means he's taking yearlings for sale. Another big trip coming up. I watch as he saddles his horse outside the barn and heads off to the north field.

I hustle the girls inside and promise to take them this afternoon to see if the shooting stars have blossomed.

When lunch is finished, I put Lucy and Bella down for a nap and read a fairy tale to Helen. She needs to learn her alphabet. She's starting to count too, but we need to keep practising.

It's a long afternoon. If Mama were here, we'd have a cup of tea together. I'd never make tea just for myself.

When Lucy wakes up, I put in the girls in sweaters and carry Bella for a walk by the creek. The air is gentle, but the path is muddy.

The water's running high now after the spring rains, and the grass on the bank is slippery. "Be careful. Stay on the path," I tell the girls.

A short way down the path Helen calls, "Look, Anna!" She points to a cluster of pale purple flowers under a tree. "I found them! Mama's shooting stars."

Helen and Lucy are on their knees close to the small blossoms hanging upside-down from their slender stems.

"Me see," Lucy says.

Helen tugs my arm. "She's talking!"

"Clever girl, Lucy." I ruffle her hair as she bends to the flowers.

I dip Bella down to see too. I'm happy to be here, showing the girls things that were important to Mama.

"Why are they upside-down?" Helen asks.

"Mama always said they're like stars shooting down from the sky. Let's see how many you can count, Helen."

Helen touches the tops of each one as she counts. "One, two, three, four, five, six, seven, eight, nine, ten... What's next, Anna?"

Lucy bursts in, "On, too... uh-hum!"

Helen grins at me. She's so good to her little sister, but it must be frustrating at times. She's only four years old and has two sisters younger than she is. Then she looks serious. "Is Mama in Heaven now, Anna?"

I don't know how to answer her. I don't even know if there is a place called Heaven, though the Church taught me there was.

I squat down beside the girls. I want my answer to give them comfort. "Mama's in a safe place. She's warm and she's happy. Maybe she's watching us now when we're counting shooting stars."

"I miss Mama. I don't know why she died," Helen says.

"Mama," Lucy says, "Mama." Tears roll over her round cheeks.

Why did our mother die? Was she wrong to get pregnant again? Is it Papa's fault? Should I have known she was slipping away when I sat with her that night? What could I have done?

I can't answer the girls. Tears are pushing at my own eyes. Then the girls are up and running ahead down the path. Lucy, who's still not that steady on her feet, stops to peer over the bank of the creek.

As I'm watching, she slips over the bank and topples into the water. Still holding Bella, I run down to the bank to reach her. With my free hand, I grab the back of her sweater and pull her out of the water.

Lucy is wet and heavy, but I manage to pull her partway up the bank. With more effort, I lift her onto the path where she sits, too frightened to cry. Helen is screaming. Bella has felt the scare and is crying too.

Lucy might have been swept away in the water. How could I have rescued her while I was holding Bella?

Lucy stares at me, wide-eyed, her face white with shock. Her clothes are slick from the cold mud, and both her shoes and mine are black with it.

The scare has made me shaky, but I speak as calmly as I can to the girls. "We're all safe now. Everyone is safe. Stay here on the path with me. We'll hold hands on the way home."

Lucy takes my free hand and Helen holds her other hand as we start back along the path to the house.

But *are* these girls safe? Can I keep them safe until they're grown up? It frightens me to think of what could have happened. Lucy could have drowned.

As we reach the house, Papa comes from the barn to meet us. We must be a sight, covered in mud, the scare still on our faces, holding tightly to each other's hands.

Papa's about to say something when the boys come up the road from school behind us. Joe's ahead of Berny, who kicks the dirt with every step.

"What is the matter, Berny?" Papa says.

"Damn teacher thinks I should be able to read a whole book in one day," Berny says.

"No swearing, Berny." Papa puts his arm around Berny and walks beside him up the road.

I hear Berny say, "*You* swear, Papa."

Joe picks Lucy up. "What happened to you?" He starts to laugh. "Who's been playing in the mud?"

"Not playing, Joey," Helen says. "Falling."

"Lucy slipped into the creek," I tell him. "Both the girls are cold and wet."

Joe surprises me. "We'll help you clean up, Anna."

oooooo

THE GIRLS ARE in their nightgowns and quiet at the supper table. Papa turns to us and says, "I must take cows to stockyard in Stoddart to sell this week."

"How long will you be away?" Joe asks.

"Three days. No longer."

I tell him he needs to buy flour or we won't have any bread.

"I will shop when I come back. There will be money."

Joe nudges me and says quietly, "As long as he doesn't drink it all away."

Maggie

FRIDAY, MAY 14,
AND SATURDAY, MAY 15

IT'S SCHOOL ASSEMBLY and the weekly announcements this morning. Our principal strides to the stage, straightens up, and runs his hand over the front of his pants. He does it every time to make sure he hasn't left his fly open. Jerry looks at me and raises his eyebrows.

"What a jerk!" I whisper.

Jerry's eyes crinkle at the corners. For the rest of the morning we grin every time we look at each other.

At lunchtime, Carolyn comes up to me and asks why I'm eating alone. "You can eat with me if you want. Now that you don't have the poor country girl to eat with."

"Are you referring to Anna?" I say.

"Well, she's the only one of your friends who lives on a farm. And it's not hard to tell with those shabby clothes she wears."

"How dare you say that! It doesn't matter what anyone wears!" The words explode out of me. "Anna is the smartest girl in the class. She beats you in every subject, and you know it!"

"Well, that brother of hers, Berny, isn't very smart. I heard he can hardly read."

"Berny is *so* smart, and he's a good kid. You're a snob."

Carolyn keeps trying, but there's nothing she can do to make me like her more than I like Anna. Anna is the true friend of my heart.

Carolyn sails off in a huff, her chin in the air. My heart is pounding, and I know my voice was too loud, because Jerry stares over at me from the table where he's eating lunch.

Later, he crosses the room and sits down beside me. "Good one with Carolyn."

"I try."

"Have you finished your project?"

"Got it in today. I missed Anna's help. I wrote the report in a rush and it ended up messy."

"When's Anna coming back to school?"

"She has to stay home to look after her little sisters and the baby."

"Will she ever come back?"

"Maybe not until the baby grows up." For the first time I realize how long that will be.

"That's terrible."

"It isn't fair."

"What's fair anyway?" Jerry says. "How about going for a bike ride on Saturday? I'm doing my project on coyotes and I want to see some. I thought we could take the hill by the upper field."

Sounds like my kind of adventure. "Sure. I'll bring my four sharp eyes."

Jerry laughs at that.

If you wear glasses you might as well make fun of them.

After lunch, Miss Alexander assigns us a book report to write. We settle down with our notebooks. I'm in the middle of writing a sentence when an eraser flies through the air and hits the blackboard with a thump. I saw it come from the side of the room, but I didn't see who threw it. Miss Alexander picks up the eraser, a look of surprise on her face. She looks at Carolyn, who sits across from me.

"Your name is on this eraser, Carolyn. I'm shocked that you would throw an eraser."

"I didn't, Miss Alexander," Carolyn protests. "I didn't throw it."

I know she didn't. I'm sitting right across from her and I saw the eraser come from over by the windows. In fact, from Jerry's row.

"Who did throw this eraser?" Miss Alexander asks.

No one answers. The room is electric.

Miss Alexander sighs and says, "Stay after school, Carolyn."

Carolyn puts her hands over her face to hide her crying. I know she didn't throw it. I should say something.

"Back to work everyone," Miss Alexander says.

Then it's too late for me to speak up.

••••••

"WHERE ARE YOU and Jerry going on your bikes?" Mom asks.

"Just around town," I say.

"Be home for lunch, please," Mom says. "Noon. Sharp."

"Okay, Mom. I'm wearing my watch."

She could say, "Have a good time." But that wouldn't be my mother.

Jerry and I meet in the lane behind the barracks garage.

"Hey, almost twin bikes," Jerry says, pointing to my bike. It's a CCM like his, but mine is red and his is green.

He leads the way across a bridge over the river that runs north of the barracks. A row of narrow trees, bare against the sky, march like giant skeletons along the far side of the river. They remind me of my foot bones inside the x-ray machine in the Front Street shoe store. It's amazing to be able to see through your skin to your bones. It's like looking inside a man who seems completely normal and seeing what's hidden underneath. Even the fact that he murdered his own baby.

We ride beside the river and head up the bumpy gravel road, standing on our bike pedals and pumping hard with the wind sharp in our faces. Jerry's hair blows back, making it look as though he's swimming. The wind pushes against me, and my legs feel strong as I pedal hard.

Out of breath, we stop. Jerry suggests we cut through the hay field. We lift our bikes over the fence and ride along the bumpy tire tracks left by the farmer's tractor. Light-coloured hay stretches into the distance. The sun has broken through the clouds, dappling in light and shadow across the field of blond hay.

I call to Jerry, "Don't you think it looks like yellow sand on a beach?"

"Never seen the ocean. Have you?" Jerry calls back.

"No, but I will one day!" I yell back at him.

The sun feels hot on my back as I follow Jerry. I could ride for miles and miles—until I get to the ocean.

Ahead of us, a large bird dives to the ground and then soars back into the sky.

"Hawk!" Jerry says. "Red-tailed hawk."

We keep going, stopping to catch our breath at the next fence. Across the field I spot five antelopes bending their broad necks to feed.

"Look!" I say quietly, pointing them out to Jerry. The antelopes don't notice us. We study their long black faces, the curving horns, the white bands around their tawny chests.

Jerry says, "They look so proud standing there."

I hold out my arms and whisper to them, "You're beauties." Then I wonder if Jerry thinks I sound silly.

But he opens his arms like mine and calls across to the antelopes, "We're lucky to see you here today."

Suddenly, the antelopes turn and run, bounding across the field. Their hind ends flash white as they twist like braiding around each other until they're out of sight over the next curve.

And we're alone. We lean against our bikes, with nothing but the expanse of field and sky around us, and I feel my heart opening. The way the minister at Gram's funeral said it would. It's as though my heart has grown wider, wide enough to be sad and still have space for this feeling of awe at being so close to these wild animals.

Oh, Gram. Gram.

I turn my head and hope that Jerry doesn't see me wipe my eyes. I want to keep this special feeling tight inside me.

Jerry pulls two apples out of his pack and tosses one to me. I crunch into the apple and the sweet juice bursts in my mouth. I eat right down to the core and spit the seeds into the air.

Deep Creek is spread out below us. The streets in town are laid out like crossed ladders, the three grain elevators sticking up like toy blocks. A line of dust on the far side marks the east road out of town. This is where we're from, this small, tidy place that looks like a toy town, a place where little children run their play cars. And I'm standing here beside a boy with no one else around.

"You've got a little brother, haven't you?" Jerry spits his seeds farther than mine.

"Tommy. He's one big pain in the neck."

"I wouldn't mind having a brother. It's no fun being an only child."

"He's all yours."

"Give the kid a break," Jerry says.

I change the subject. "Did you know a murderer tried to commit suicide underneath my bedroom?"

"I heard my mother talking about that guy! She said he shot his wife and threw his baby in the well. He couldn't live with what he'd done, so he tried to kill himself."

"I feel sick to my stomach thinking about that. Killing a baby—a baby like Anna's—so small and helpless. And in a well where some people drown kittens!"

"I think it's neat you live on top of criminals," Jerry says.

"Bank robbers are okay, but murderers are creepy."

Actually, I don't like either of them, but I have to live up to my status as a policeman's daughter.

I look at Jerry. "Did you throw the eraser at school yesterday?"

"No, it was Ernie beside me. What a jerk."

"I felt sorry for Carolyn. She was upset."

"I thought you didn't like her."

"I don't much."

"She only had to stay after school. No big deal." Jerry shrugs and turns back to cross the field.

I don't think I should tell him that I knew it wasn't Carolyn and didn't say anything.

We lift our bikes over the fence and we're back on the road to town. I jump on and pedal down the hill ahead of Jerry. Going fast like this, I feel strong enough to conquer the world.

When we get to the lane I look at my watch and see it's almost twelve-thirty. "I'd better go."

Jerry looks at me shyly and says, "I still want to see those coyotes. Feel like going out again?"

"Sure do," I say.

••••••

BACK IN THE house, Mom's top lip is tight. I know what that means.

"Have you forgotten how to tell time, Maggie?"

"Sorry, Mom. We had such a great ride and we saw five beautiful antelopes!"

"Antelope. The word *antelope* is plural as well as singular. Five antelope. You said you and Jerry were just riding around town."

"We decided to go to the hill at the top field instead. It wasn't far."

"You're late for lunch. Wash your hands."

I wish she'd ask me about the antelopes instead of correcting my grammar.

Instead she says, "I got a call from Mrs. Dougherty. The music examiner from the Toronto Conservatory of Music will be in Deep Creek next week. You'll have to practise twice a day now until the exam."

"I'm ready for the exam, Mom. I don't need any more practice."

"Not the way your scales sounded this morning."

I say it quietly, but I say it. "You're mean."

"I heard that," she says. "It was rude."

I decide that when I'm in the house, I have to do what Mom says. But when I'm out riding my bike, I can do whatever I want. And I can think whatever I want. I'll call them antelopes if I want to.

oooooo

LATER, I TAKE our encyclopedia to bed and read about pronghorn antelope. They can run sixty miles an hour. Even baby pronghorns can run faster than a human being. I'll tell Jerry that when we go biking again.

Through my window I can see new leaves starting to open on the big maple tree. Another spring is coming. It's three years since we came to Deep Creek, and so much has happened. I made best friends with Anna and now I never see her. Gram, my special Gram, has died and I'll never see her again. And I've become even more confused wondering if I really am adopted. In one way, I badly want to find out, but in another way, I don't want it to be true. It would change everything. And one thing bothers me. How could I explain feeling so close to Dad?

At least I have a bike ride to look forward to. It suits the adventurous spirit in me. I want to see new things, to ride fast and take chances. I have a new friend who likes adventures too. And my new friend is a boy.

I fall asleep dreaming of riding to the top of the hill, standing next to Jerry and watching the elegant antelope in their winding dance across the golden field.

Anna

TUESDAY, MAY 18

I HEAR A car drive up early in the morning and look out to see two women wearing hats walking up to the door. My heart sinks. It's the church ladies. Mama was on their list of people to visit and now they've come to check on *me*. How dare those women come snooping around, clucking like old hens and judging what they see in our house. I don't want their sympathy.

The girls are still at the breakfast table in their night-gowns. I'm tempted to pretend no one is home when they knock, but Helen and Lucy run to the door and open it. The church ladies, white gloves and all, are inspecting the peeling paint on the side of the house.

"Aren't you cuties?" they say to Helen and Lucy.

Lucy reaches up for the parcel one woman is holding.

"What did you bring us?" Helen asks.

"That's not polite," I say, moving the girls to the side. "Sorry. We don't have visitors very often."

"I'm Mrs. Harris and this is Mrs. Hayes," says the woman with the parcel. She's wearing a tall round hat that looks like a bird's nest. She walks right into the kitchen.

"We brought you oatmeal cookies," says Mrs. Hayes, smiling at the girls. Her hat is orange with a green feather sticking out of the top.

"Can we have a cookie now?" Helen asks.

Mrs. Harris frowns. "I think not. You should wait until after lunch."

Helen sulks, and then grabs Lucy's hand and leads her over to play with the cat on the floor.

"Come and sit down." I point to the worn couch in our living room, which is really just part of the kitchen. They sit side by side, as stiff as fence posts, adjusting their skirts.

I don't intend to offer them tea. I remember another visit of church women when Mama served tea. I saw them exchange looks over the chipped cups.

"This is Bella," I say. I turn Bella on my lap so they can see her.

"A dear baby," says Mrs. Hayes.

"Is she sleeping through the night?" Mrs. Harris asks.

They're not going to find out anything to spread around town. "Oh yes, she does. She hardly ever cries," I assure them.

Helen bursts in. "She cries a whole lot. We don't mind. We love her."

"Owie," Lucy says. She points to a purple bruise on her forehead.

"Did you hurt your head, little girl?" Mrs. Hayes says.

Helen says, "Her name's Lucy."

"Lucy had a small fall," I say. I'm not going to tell them that two days ago Lucy fell partway down the stairs and screamed for half an hour. "She's fine. She bruises easily."

Mrs. Hayes stops staring at Lucy and turns to me. "Are you managing all right, Anna? You don't have anyone to help, do you?"

"Oh, yes. Papa and the boys. When the boys get home from school they help with everything."

"Your Papa's around in the day, is he?"

"Can we have a cookie now?" Helen asks.

Lucy pushes herself up from the floor. "Uh-hum."

I stand too. "I'd better feed Bella. She's due for her bottle."

The women get up from the sofa, and Mrs. Harris says, "Is there anything we can do for you?" She straightens her awful hat and looks at the door.

I shake my head. I can't see either of them hauling water and washing dirty diapers wearing their hats and good dresses. It's not as if they'd get down on their knees and scrub the kitchen floor.

"You know," says Mrs. Hayes, "if it's too difficult for you to care for the new baby, the Welfare Department can put her in a foster home. That is, if they feel you can't manage."

What? I'd never heard of that. Surely no one could take Bella away from us!

Papa wouldn't allow it. *I* wouldn't allow it.

I try to make my voice sound confident. "We're managing very well. We miss Mama, of course, but I have lots of help. Thank you for coming."

They're out the door and driving away before I can steady my breath. I saw them looking at the dirty dishes on the table and the girls still in their nightgowns. I'm sure they'll gossip all over town. If that's what people who go to church do, I never intend to go back.

When I'm certain the car's gone, I dress the girls and take them outside with me while I hang up the diapers. There's just enough sun to get them dry.

The girls and I play tag. Poor little Lucy keeps tripping when she tries to run and she doesn't get the "hide" part of hide and seek. She stands there in plain view, covering her eyes and thinking I can't see her. Helen gets it and pulls Lucy behind the washing shed with her. Then I pretend to find them both.

A wonderful thing happens while we're outside. I hear it first and then see it. Circling high above us is not a hawk, but the first spring meadowlark. With the song I love, the lark's beautiful bubbly whistle. The meadowlark circles around, coming lower and lower to land on the post near our barn, so close we can see the black necklace on the bird's yellow breast.

"Do you hear that song?" I ask the girls. "Mama used to say the meadowlark was sending a message."

Helen asks, "What does the message say?"

"It says, *I was here a year ago. I was here a year ago.* Can you hear it?"

"I think I can," Helen says.

We watch until the meadowlark flies back up into the sky and disappears.

After lunch, I put Bella in her cradle and lie down for a sleep on the couch with the girls. Thoughts of the Welfare Department taking Bella away keep me awake.

There's a knock on the door. I freeze. Have the church ladies come back with someone from the Welfare Department? I didn't hear a car. It must be Mrs. Covey who's walked over from her place.

It is. And she's brought some wooden blocks her boys have finished playing with.

"I thought Helen and Lucy would like them," she says. "I'll put the water on for tea, shall I?"

"I'll get Bella's bottle ready."

I wipe the girls' noses and settle them down in the corner to play with the blocks.

"Thanks, Mrs. Covey. The girls don't have blocks."

I pour the tea, and Mrs. Covey says, "Let me feed Bella so you can enjoy your tea."

I know Mama liked Mrs. Covey and they had things in common, both of them living in the country with farmers for husbands. I decide to tell her what's bothering me.

"Mrs. Covey, do you think the Welfare Department could come and take Bella away?

"Where did you get that idea?" she says.

"Two women from the church said it could happen."

"I wouldn't worry about it."

"I've been worrying about it ever since they told me this morning."

Mrs. Covey looks at me across the table. "Anna, you look worn out. How are you doing?"

I don't expect these kind words, and the awful day has made me weepy. Tears of self-pity flood my eyes.

"It's hard," I say. "I'm tired. In fact, I'm exhausted. I'm beginning to think Bella's crying in the night means she has colic. Papa's been away for two days, and I'm not sure when he'll get back. The boys don't do one more thing around here than they have to."

Now I've let it all out to Mrs. Covey. A big mistake. I take a gulp of my cold tea. Her grey eyes look concerned. Mrs. Covey's older than my mother was, but I've always thought she'd once been pretty. She and her husband don't have much money either, and her boy needs special shoes ordered from Toronto. She sits across from me with Bella in her arms, and I can see she's deciding what she should say.

Finally she says, "My dear girl, it breaks my heart to see you like this. You're just a child yourself."

This starts me off in a real crying jag. Helen gets up from the blocks and comes over, leans into me, and pats my arm. Lucy takes the opportunity to knock down the block house Helen was building.

"Down!"

Another word. That makes us smile, and I wipe my eyes on my sleeve.

"It's terrible your father can't get someone to help you, Anna," Mrs. Covey says. "I'd take the girls over to my place today, but two of my kids have mumps. I don't want you to have to deal with that."

"You have your hands full, Mrs. Covey. I know that."

"What about your school work? Can you do that at night?"

"I want to, but by the time the girls are in bed I'm too tired. My teacher brought my books. But they just sit here. I won't be able to pass grade seven."

"It will be better when your father gets back, won't it, Anna?"

"Not much. Papa's either out with the cows or in town." I don't mention that he sometimes comes home a bit drunk, but everyone around here seems to know that anyway. I wonder again if Maggie knows.

"Anna, my dear," says Mrs. Covey, putting Bella down in the cradle, "I wish I could help. But honestly, I think you have to carry on and do the best you can."

"I'll be all right. I'm sorry I told you all this." I've let my guard down and told Mrs. Covey too much. I try to smile. "Things aren't that bad most of the time."

She gives me a doubtful smile as she goes to the door. "Your mother would be real proud of you, Anna."

She waves at us as we stand in the doorway watching her walk along the road to her own house.

Joe and Berny pass Mrs. Covey as they come up the road from school. They follow us inside and pile their books on the kitchen table.

"Would you boys bring in more wood, please?" I ask.

"Let Berny do it," Joe says. "I brought in a load yesterday."

"You do it!" Berny yells. "Stop bossing me around."

"I milk Dover morning and night," Joe says, "and I've got a load of homework. It's no joke being in grade ten, you know."

"Oh, poor Joe. Poor old Joe," Berny says.

"At least I do my school work. I never see you doing any. How's your reading coming?"

Berny grimaces and says, "I'll smash you for that." He lashes out at Joe, hitting him in the arm. Joe makes a fist and hits back, getting Berny on the shoulder. Berny tries to hit Joe's jaw but misses.

The girls stop playing with the blocks and stare at their brothers.

"Stop it, you two!" I shout. "You're upsetting the girls."

The boys wrestle back and forth, grunting and yelling, then crumpling to the floor. They sit, catching their breath and muttering at each other.

I'm shaking with anger. "Neither one of you is any help around here. I used the last of the wood at breakfast. It's been freezing cold in the house all day. And the girls have colds. Didn't you hear Helen coughing last night?"

They don't often hear me so angry.

"Sorry," Berny says.

"I'm sorry too, Sis," Joe says.

"It's so thoughtless of you. You expect to come home and have a hot dinner ready and your laundry done. It's not right that I have do everything around here. It's especially not fair that I'm home all day while you two are at school."

"Come on, Berny," Joe says. "We'll both get the wood."

"We'll get enough to last two days, Anna," Berny says, grinning at me.

I don't smile back. "Thank you."

After supper, Joe and Berny clear the table and do the dishes. It's cozy in the kitchen, and Joe does his homework at the kitchen table. Berny plays with the girls and then sits with a book on his lap.

At midnight, when Bella finishes her bottle, I'm exhausted. I wipe the milk off her cheek and stroke it with my finger. Bella smiles. Her first smile. She's smiling at me! As though I'm her real mama! Well, I guess I'm the only mother she knows.

FRIDAY, MAY 21, AND SATURDAY, MAY 22

IT'S ANNA'S BIRTHDAY next Thursday—her thirteenth birthday—and I want to get out to the farm to see her. The problem is, I need a ride. I'll ask Dad as soon as soon as he gets home from Regina. He probably doesn't want any more to do with Mr. Lozowski, though.

I want to give Anna something special. I don't have money to buy anything, and I don't want to try knitting another scarf. I lie in bed thinking about what to get until Mom calls me for a final piano practice. The exam is tomorrow morning.

I sigh and force myself to the piano bench.

Mom says, "Don't you *care* how you do on the exam?"

"Actually, I don't, Mom."

The important thing to me right now is to see Anna for her birthday. I can't think of anything else.

"Get practising and put your mind to it."

I pound away at the pieces for a whole hour. Every time I strike a key I'm more certain than ever that she can't be my real mother. My real mother would smile and tell me I already play these pieces perfectly.

Dad came back from Regina this afternoon. Before dinner, he tells Mom that the prisoner is healed enough to stand trial.

I grab his arm. "Will he be in jail?"

"Probably in the mental institution over in Weyburn." Dad puts his arm around me. "He's a sick man, Mags. No need for you to worry about him."

"I do think about him, Dad. I can't figure out what's going on in his head."

"The doctors in the institution will help him sort himself out."

"I sure hope so." I take a breath. "Dad, I've been waiting to ask you something important. Could you please drive me to see Anna?"

"Sorry, Mags, I've been away and I'll be up to my ears in work for the next week."

"It's Anna's birthday, Dad. She's my best friend. Please, drive me." I hear my whiny voice.

Mom interrupts before Dad can answer. "Maggie, stop pestering your father and set the table. Dinner's almost ready."

She's chopping celery and apples for Dad's favourite Waldorf salad. She turns to me and says, "Carolyn's mother phoned to ask if you'd like to go to their horse farm tomorrow afternoon. I said you'd go."

"I'm not going," I say too quickly. "I've arranged a bike ride with Jerry after my music exam."

Tommy sings out, "Maggie's scared of hor-ses!"

It's true. I am a bit afraid of horses. I like watching them, but they have such big teeth. I'm afraid they'll bite. I glare at Tommy.

"Why don't you want to go?" Mom says. "You're not the best person at picking friends."

"I can pick my own friends," I mutter.

"What did you say?" She chops furiously.

"I said, I don't want to go anywhere with Carolyn."

"What do you mean, you don't want to?"

"I mean, I can't. I promised Jerry I'd go bike riding with him."

"You can go bike riding next weekend, Maggie." She scrapes the chopped apples into a bowl.

"I can't go with Carolyn, Mom." I take a huge breath. "Jerry and I are working on a geology report that's due on Wednesday. We have to find geodes and different kinds of rocks."

The lie slips out so easily. I hold my breath, waiting to see if she'll believe me.

Mom sighs. "All right. I'll phone and explain, but one day you might need Carolyn for a friend. She may never invite you again."

That sounds too good to be true. Then I remember letting Carolyn take the blame for throwing the eraser. I rush to my room to drive away the guilty feeling.

Oh, Gram, I hope you're not sitting up there in Heaven hearing me lie. I can't miss the bike ride.

••••••

AT DINNER, TOMMY is more stupid than ever.

"Knock-knock."

Another one of his dumb jokes.

"Who's there?" Mom says.

"Police."

"Police who?"

"Pu-lease don't put me in jail. I've been good."

He's giggling over a joke he's told us about a hundred times before. It probably goes over well with the kindergarten kids, but it's totally stale with me.

"Why aren't you laughing?" Tommy pokes me in the arm.

"Ha. Very funny."

"Laugh harder, Maggie Waggy!"

That drives me mad, and I poke him back.

"She hit me," Tommy wails.

"Stop it, you two," Dad says.

I leave the room and walk through the apartment, trying to think what I can get for Anna's birthday. And even if I do think of the right thing, how can I take it out to her?

oooooo

ON SATURDAY MORNING, Mom walks with me to the music examination room and waits outside when my name is called. Mrs. Dougherty sits at the back of the room with a sour look on her face.

I'm feeling nervous, but the examiner is an older man who starts off by saying, "Just relax and we'll start with a G Major scale."

When it's over, the examiner thanks me. Outside the room, Mrs. Dougherty says to Mom, "Well, she probably passed."

On the way home, Mom says, "See, all that practising paid off for you."

Maybe if I'd failed, Mom would let me stop taking lessons. Wish I'd thought of that.

oooooo

WHEN JERRY AND I meet in the afternoon, I'm so happy I challenge him to a race up the hill. We get to the top at the same time, arriving breathless at the fence, and grin at each other. As we're cutting across the field, Jerry stops and points silently.

It's a grey coyote. The coyote lopes through the field, his shoulders hunched low, tail down. But the movement of Jerry's hand alarms the coyote, and he bolts off to the crest of the hill. Then, keeping his body pointed away, the coyote stops and turns his head back. He stands silhouetted on the hill, boldly watching us.

"Look, he's daring us to come after him," Jerry says.

"Sort of nervy."

"They are nervy."

Then we see another coyote come loping over the crest of the hill. "I was waiting for it," Jerry tells me. "Probably his mate. Coyotes hunt in pairs. They're hungry and looking for rabbits and gophers."

We watch as the two coyotes stare proudly across at us, almost like they're challenging us to acknowledge them. Then they turn and amble slowly over the rise.

"I like coyotes," Jerry says. "They're not like other animals, because they don't run away. They just stand and stare you down. Coyotes are fearless and free."

On our way back down the road, the sky is streaked with fast-moving clouds, the feathery wisps announcing a change in the weather. Jerry suggests we ride to the place where the river loops away from the town, which means we cross another field on a narrow track down to the river. The path is steep, and I'm scared that my brakes won't hold, but I keep up with Jerry and skid to a shaky stop at the bank above the water.

We drop our bikes and find seats on a flat rock. I stretch my bare legs out along the warm rock. I cringe at the way my legs look. They're almost as white as my ankle socks. I pass Jerry the oatmeal cookies I've brought with me.

All of a sudden he cups his hand under his armpit and pumps his arm. A sharp farting noise erupts in the air. I laugh, and so does Jerry. It's the first time I've noticed how white his teeth are.

"Show me how to do that," I say.

I practise until I can make farting sounds too. It's especially funny to hear that sound out here with no one around to hear. We make the noise as loud and as often as we want.

Jerry starts looking for something near the bank. He takes out a jackknife and cuts the stem of a tall plant and cleans off the leaves.

"See how porous they are? They'll make good cigarettes."

"You think we can smoke them?"

"For sure. I've got matches."

"How'd you get matches?"

"I just take them."

Wow. Jerry's got nerve.

He cuts the stem into two cigarette lengths, and we light up. The stem is so dry it flares out, almost setting fire to my bangs.

I hold my cigarette like Mom, in the air between my first and second fingers and tip it up. Then I stick out my bottom lip and puff. The cigarettes mostly taste of grass, but they're so dry, it's impossible to keep them lit, no matter how hard I pull. It's hard to feel sophisticated when you're puffing on a dry stem.

Jerry and I talk about the end of school and the summer holidays coming up, then lie back and watch the clouds.

"It would be great to have real cigarettes," I say.

He looks at me. "Dare you to get some."

I think about it. There are always cigarettes in the tin on our kitchen shelf. "I accept your dare!"

I don't know why I do this, but I turn to him and say, "I dare you to kiss me." I read in a book about a girl saying this to a boy, but it's a shock to hear the words come out of my own mouth.

"I accept," Jerry says. He leans over and plants his lips on mine. It feels different from the way I imagined it would. Different in a good way. Warm.

I turn away and drop my eyes. Anna would never do something like that. I'd better change the subject. "It's Anna's birthday next week, and I badly want to see her. Dad can't give me a ride."

"Why not ride your bike out to the farm?"

"Mom would never let me ride that far. She'd have a fit."

"Do you have to tell her?"

"I guess I don't."

It's actually a good idea. Why can't I go out to see Anna if it's important to me? It means another lie to Mom, but I'll do it. I like Jerry's ideas. We're both coyotes, fearless and free.

"I'll ride with you on the road out," he says, "but I won't go into Anna's house. I don't know what to say to her about her mother dying. You can go in and I'll turn back. Are you okay to ride back by yourself?"

"Sure. How about tomorrow afternoon?"

"Fine. That's settled."

Coming down the hill we go slowly. The wind is stronger now, and pink-tipped grasses flap wildly at the side of the road. Jerry is riding ahead of me, and suddenly he brakes sharply. As I get closer, he picks something up from the middle of the road. I'm horrified to see a small dead bird cupped in his hand.

"Poor thing. Probably flew into a car," Jerry says. "There's not a mark on it."

"It's a baby meadowlark," I say as I stroke its soft back.

We look closely at the bird's pale yellow breast with the thin black necklace. The bird's beak is closed, its dark eyes open, glistening in the sunlight but seeing nothing.

That's what being dead looks like. I think of Gram lying cold and dead in the graveyard. I think of Anna's mother too. How can any of us be happy when we know what death is? Something has gone from your life forever.

Jerry carries the bird to the side of the road. We lay a blanket of grasses over the small body and stand looking at it. This baby bird was alive one minute and dead the next. Something has left it. Is that what death means?

I wonder if some part of a living being goes on. Maybe part of Anna's mother will be inside Anna forever. The part that makes her so loving with the little girls. And inside me are all the memories I have of Gram. Special things I can remember.

I'm lost in the thoughts going around in my head when I hear a loud farting noise come from Jerry.

"Come on. Stop looking so down in the dumps. You and I won't be dead for a long time! Let's go!" He starts down the hill.

He's right. I wouldn't want Gram to look down from Heaven and see me being sad. I can have adventures and laugh at things and still keep the memory of her alive inside me.

At the gate behind the barracks, Jerry says, "How about showing me the cell where the prisoner was."

"Sure. Let's go now."

We stash our bikes by the garage, and I check that Otto's nowhere around. The door to the cells is next to the bottom of our stairs.

I warn Jerry to be quiet as we go inside. The cells are empty, with the thick padlocks hanging loose on the doors.

I swing open the heavy door to the nearest cell. Not much in it except a metal cot with a thin mattress on wooden slats, a stained pillow, a sink, and a toilet without a seat. There's a sour smell coming from the toilet. Jerry goes inside and sits on the bed. Then he lies down with his head on the pillow.

"Let's see what it feels like with the door shut," Jerry says.

I want to show him that I'm no chicken. I grab the metal bars and swing the door closed with a loud clang, checking first to make sure the padlock doesn't close.

Jerry slides over to make room for me on the sagging mattress. "Come and lie down."

I try hard not to touch any part of him. I leave one foot on the floor to keep from falling off the mattress. This is the first time I've been inside a cell. The first time I've been beside a boy on a bed. My throat feels tight.

"Not such a bad place to hang out," Jerry says.

"Not bad." I feel strange. Any second now I'll roll right off. Maybe Jerry will be my boyfriend. I should know more about him.

I clear my throat. "What's your full name?"

"Jerrard Edward. After my uncle."

"Jerry's better than Jerrard."

"What's yours?

"Margaret Rose. After the princess."

Jerry laughs. "I prefer Maggie."

"My dad calls me Mags," I say, shifting my head to look at him. Then I feel embarrassed and say, "Right here is where the murderer tried to kill himself."

"Oh boy! My mom says she heard he got a knife somehow and tried to slit his wrists."

This creeps me out. We both sit up. We inspect the walls and the floor.

"I don't see any blood stains," I say, standing up.

Jerry stands too, looking around. "I guess the janitor cleaned them up."

"Dad says the prisoner will probably be sent to the mental institution over in Weyburn. He says he's mentally ill."

"More like a guilty conscience, I'd say."

"I don't know about that. I heard him crying."

"No kidding,"

"Yes. I snuck down, but I didn't actually see him. Just heard him crying. I can't figure out why. I mean, how can you kill two people, people you should love, and then turn around and cry about it?"

"Confused in his head. That's mental illness, I guess."

"I guess. We'd better go," I say.

Back outside I can breathe again. We go around by the garage and make plans to meet tomorrow after lunch for the ride out to Anna's. At the gate, Tommy calls, "Don't forget the dare!"

I think he means his dare for me to get cigarettes, not my dare for him to kiss me, but I'm not sure. I go back up the stairs.

Now all I have to do is figure out what to take Anna and how to explain another bike ride with Jerry tomorrow. I'll tell Mom that Jerry and I are still looking for geodes and we won't be gone long.

••••••

I LIE IN bed with my mind going through all the things in my room, thinking of what I can give Anna. I could take her some of my books, but they're secondhand and I don't know how much time she has to read. I could take her one of my best sweaters, but Mom would notice it was gone.

My eyes land on the china bluebird on my dresser. It would be hard for me to give away something Gram gave me. Something so special. But I remember reading that a gift is only worth giving if it's something you truly love yourself. I do love this china bird, and I love Anna too. And she doesn't have anything special for herself.

Gram would understand.

The little bird would be something to give Anna hope—hope that things will be easier some day. I fall asleep with a warm feeling inside me.

I've found the perfect present.

Anna

SUNDAY, MAY 23

LUCY TIPPED THE potty over when she stood up. I've just cleaned up the mess when Joe comes in from the yard, tracking his muddy boots over the kitchen floor.

"Joe, take off your boots and clean up the mud!"

"Sorry, crabby Annie," he says, getting a rag. He gives the floor a half-hearted wipe, throws the rag in the corner, and grabs a piece of bread. He smears honey on it and heads outside again. His mood matches mine today.

I have a sore throat and feel I'm catching the girls' colds. Both of them coughed all last night. It's cloudy today but not raining, and so I decide to hang the diapers outside.

I put Bella in her cradle, where she sucks away happily at her thumb. I dump the box of blocks on the floor for Helen and Lucy. "Stay here and play. Call me if Bella cries," I tell them.

Outside, it's warmer than I expected, with a good wind to blow the diapers, like a row of grey flags. Long thin clouds stream through the sky, and the wind is warm on my face. I'm looking out at the fields when I hear someone calling my name.

Am I dreaming or is that Maggie coming down the driveway on her bike?

I run to meet her. "Maggie, you rode all the way out here!"

She's out of breath, but smiling, the freckles standing out across her nose and her cheeks bright red. "I had to see you. Jerry rode out from town with me, but he turned back at the highway."

"He could have come in."

"He says hi. He's not sure what to say to you about your mother." She leans her bike against the house and catches her breath.

"I'm so glad to see you," I tell her, giving her a hug. "Miss Alexander told me about your grandmother. I'm so sorry."

"I miss her a lot, Anna."

"I miss my mother too."

We go inside, and Maggie makes a fuss over the girls. Helen shows her the blocks, and Maggie says, "Can I build something with you?"

"Uh-hum," says Lucy, sliding over and pulling Maggie down beside her on the floor. They build happily while

I wash the pile of dishes. Bella wakes up and starts to fuss in her cradle.

Maggie calls out, "Can I get her?"

She picks Bella up and sits holding her at the kitchen table.

"Oh, she's just smiled at me!" she says.

"She's been smiling for a while."

"She's beautiful. And she's growing so fast. I just bent over to give her a kiss and she tried to grab my glasses. She's strong!"

"I know. She kicks her legs all the time when she's beside me in bed. I hold her close and we fall back asleep."

Maggie plays patty cake with Bella and looks across the table at me. "You're taking good care of her, Anna."

"It's hard sometimes, but I'm keeping my promise to Mama."

"The girls are happy too," Maggie says.

I watch them playing together in the living room. "Maggie, I worry that maybe someone from the Welfare Department can take Bella away."

"What makes you think that?"

I lower my voice so the girls don't hear. "Two church ladies came to the house last week. They said if I couldn't manage with Bella, she'd be taken away."

"Oh, that would never happen. Bella's part of your family. No outsider can split up a family," Maggie says.

She sounds so sure. I hope she's right. Maggie looks over at the girls and says, "Why don't we have a proper tea party today?"

"Yes!" Helen shouts.

"Uh-hum!" says Lucy.

"Good idea," I say as I slide the saucepan onto the stove and reach for Mama's cups. Maggie won't mind that they're chipped.

We sit around the kitchen table. Maggie talks in a grown-up lady's voice. "Shall I pour?" The girls giggle and pass their cups. Maggie and I speak like women at a tea party in a game of pretend that my mother used to play with me.

"Care for sugar in your tea?" Maggie asks the girls.

"I'd like two spoonfuls, please," Helen says. She stirs her tea carefully.

"Me." Lucy lifts her cup and spills the tea.

Sitting here at the kitchen table makes me think of Mama. She'd call me for tea and let out a big sigh as she lowered herself onto a chair. I'd watch her take a long sip, her thin fingers circling the cup, her brown eyes loving as she smiled across at me.

Helen is chatting away, completely into playing the grown-up, and asks Maggie, "And why are you wearing glasses, Maggie?"

"Because I need them to see things properly." She leans over and tickles Helen and then Lucy. "I couldn't see both of YOU if I didn't have glasses!"

Helen has another question. "Do you have a sister, Maggie?"

"I have a brother," Maggie says.

"Do you play with him?"

"Not much."

I notice she changes the subject.

"Such fine weather we're having, isn't it? I do believe spring is on the way."

"We saw Mommy's favourite shooting stars!" Helen says.

"Fwowwrs," Lucy adds, tea dripping down her blouse.

"Will you take me to see them?" Maggie smiles at the girls.

Maggie makes everything fun. I can feel myself relaxing.

"Why don't you have a break, Anna?" she says. "I'll take Bella and the girls out."

I'm not sure about this, but Maggie's already putting sweaters on the excited girls.

She looks pleased when she sees me wrap Bella in the yellow blanket her mother made.

The girls are out the door already, leading the way.

"Watch Lucy beside the creek," I call to Maggie. "Hold her hand."

She runs after the girls. "I'll take good care of them."

It feels strange to be in the house alone. I should clean up the tea things and pick up the blocks, but I think I'll sit for a minute in Mama's old chair.

The next thing I know, Lucy and Helen are bursting in the door and I wake up. They're in high spirits after their time with Maggie. It makes me feel guilty. I've been so busy trying to keep everything together. Why don't I ever make time just to have fun with them?

"I think Bella's getting hungry," Maggie says.

Maggie sits at the kitchen table and watches me warm the milk on the stove.

"Anna, you look awfully tired."

"I've just woken up and I feel a bit dopey."

"Is there anyone to help you around the house?"

"Mrs. Covey comes over now and then for an hour."

"I want to help, Anna, but I don't know how."

"It's not up to you, Maggie. You have your own life. This is my life now. When Bella gets older it'll be easier. She'll sleep through the night and soon start eating solid food. And Helen will be in school before too long."

We settle the girls on the couch with a book and Maggie gives Bella her bottle while I heat up some soup for supper.

Maggie says, "I saw a woman in town last week. She was walking along by the Post Office. She looked like she might be my real mother."

"What do you mean?"

"She had glasses like me and she was smartly dressed in a blue suit. She seemed friendly. She smiled at me. I smiled back, but we both kept going. Now I wish I'd said something to her."

"Maggie, do you honestly think your mother isn't your real mother?"

"I'm more certain about it every day. We're so different. Mostly I think it's because she's mean to me and so nice to Tommy."

Bella's squirming, so I tell Maggie, "Pat her back to burp her. Babies are cranky when they have gas."

Maggie pats Bella's back, and I sit down beside her. "Lots of kids feel the way you do."

"Tommy looks like her, but I'm like Dad. In every way." She rubs Bella's back. "I try to imagine what my real mother is like. If she's even alive. Then I think maybe I'm making it all up."

"I don't understand why you haven't asked if you're adopted."

"I had decided to ask Gram, but she was tired when she came to stay with us. And the only time we were alone was at night when she'd fall asleep . . . and then she died."

Maggie looks so unhappy. I wish I could help. I take Bella and put her down in her cradle.

"Why not just ask your parents?"

"I think I'm afraid of their answer," Maggie says.

"Maybe it's better to know one way or the other than to keep worrying about it."

"I'm not sure." Maggie shakes her head and looks anxiously toward the door. "I should go home, it's getting late."

"Stay and have soup with us. I've got a potful. Papa will be home any minute and he'll give you a ride to town in his truck."

"He wouldn't mind?" Maggie says. "I don't like the idea of riding my bike alone."

"He'll be glad to drive you." The door bangs as I put soup in the bowls. Maggie stands up expectantly, but it's Berny and Joe. They sit down with us, and I watch the loaf of bread disappear.

"Will your dad be home soon?" Maggie's looking at the door.

"Any minute. Going with him will be faster than riding your bike." I light the kerosene lamp and help Lucy eat her soup.

Maggie's finished doing the dishes with the girls when I hear Papa's truck. The door slams, and right away I can tell by his swagger and his loud voice he's been drinking.

"How is my liddle family tonight? Who ish this pretty visitor?" He hasn't shaved for days and his hands are shaking.

"It's Maggie, Papa. She's come all the way out to spend the afternoon with me. She rode her bike and now she needs a ride back into town. Can you put her bike in the back of the truck?"

"Sure, I will do that." Papa beams at Maggie.

"Can we go now?" Maggie asks.

"First I must eat," Papa says.

Maggie looks worried. She glances out the window. Suddenly she jumps up and puts on her jacket. "It's okay, Mr. Lozowski. It won't take me long to get home."

"Wait a minute there!" Papa reaches out his arm out to stop Maggie. "I will take you. First I finish here. Got more bread, Anna?"

Before I can say anything, Maggie is going to the door. I run after her.

"Are you going? Will you be all right?"

"It's not even dark yet. I'll be home in less than an hour." She reaches into her jacket pocket and takes out a white box. "Happy birthday, Anna. You'll be thirteen next week." She hands me the box. "Older than me for six whole months."

"Thanks for remembering, Maggie." I watch the best friend I'll ever have ride away in the dwindling light to the main road.

SUNDAY, MAY 23

THERE'S ENOUGH LIGHT to see, but I don't remember the road being so rough. The noise of a car comes up behind me, the headlights flaring down the road. I wheel my bike to the side. The car stops. The driver, a middle-aged man wearing a windbreaker, leans out the window, his dark eyes looking me up and down. No one I know.

"What's a young girl like you doing out alone at this time of night?" He has an accent I don't recognize. He might be okay.

My foot is on the bike pedal as I explain. "I've been visiting a friend and it got later than I thought. Just heading back to town." I move my bike further along, careful not to slide into the ditch.

"Not a good idea," he says. "It's almost completely dark. Get in the car. I'll put your bike in the boot and we'll have you in town in no time."

"Boot." That means he's British. In English books, car trunks are called "boots." I don't know anyone in Deep Creek who speaks like that. He must be from out of town. I *do* know enough not to speak to strangers.

My wheels get traction in the gravel, and I call out, "It's okay. It won't take me long."

The man drives slowly along beside me and keeps talking out the car window.

"You're being a foolish girl. Get off your bike. I'll load it up for you and have you in town quickly." He sounds angry.

My voice comes out in rush. "Please leave me alone. My dad's the RCMP officer in town."

"Okay, girlie, but be careful. You have no lights on your bike. Cars coming along won't see you." He shakes his head, then drives away, slowly gaining speed until his car disappears from view.

It's getting darker, and I pedal as fast as I can on the gravel road. I'm shivering. My hands are cold on the metal handlebars. In my rush to leave I didn't do up my jacket, but I can't stop. I keep wondering if the stranger might turn around and come back and force me into his car.

It's much darker now, and I still can't see the town lights. Then, at the side of the road, I hear rustling noises. Huge shadows are moving around there. The shadows shuffle and shift, more solid and black than the night around them. *What are they? Are there some wild creatures out here that nobody told me about?* I hear their long, heaving breaths. My head is pounding so hard I can't think.

I'm stupid to be out here alone at night. I pedal faster, wobbling on the rough stones, and now the massive creatures are coming closer to the road. I hear a muffled lowing, and for a second, I don't recognize the sound. And then I understand. The dark shadows in the field are cows! Probably Mr. Lozowski's cows.

I'd been holding my breath and now I'm breathing too fast. *Calm down*, I tell myself. You're silly to get frightened over a bunch of cows. Some prairie girl you are.

I bend over the handlebars and I'm pedalling fast down the road when two yellow eyes flash across the front of my bike. I swerve and skid, falling with the bike almost on top of me. The animal, whatever it was, has scurried into the bushes on the other side. I crawl out from under the bike and stand up. My hand hurts. I brush at the gravel stuck to it.

The bike wheels seem to work. I climb back on, but something's wrong.

I can't see! My glasses have been knocked off. They must be lying somewhere on the road. I put the bike down and start to look for them. I grope in the road, but it's too dark to see anything. I sweep my hands in circles over the gravel, but I can't feel the glasses. Now I have to ride home without them.

Never mind, I think, as I see the town street lights, it was worth it. Anna knows I remembered her birthday and she has my present to open.

As I park my bike by the garage, I shiver. I'm in trouble. It's late. And I'm home without glasses.

Mom's at the door as soon as I open it. Her eyes look red and her voice is sharp. "Young lady, you had me scared half to death."

I'm shivering with the cold.

"What have you done with your glasses?" she says. "Has anyone hurt you?"

"No one hurt me, Mom."

"You've scraped your hand. And there's blood on your face."

I look at my hand, then reach up to touch my cheek. "I skidded off my bike on the gravel. I'm okay. But I feel terrible about losing my glasses."

Mom makes a sound like "tsk." She takes my arm and sits me down on a kitchen chair. "I'll clean you up. Stay there."

Tommy comes into the kitchen, jumping up and down with excitement. "You're going to get heck, Maggie! Nobody knew where you were."

"Shut up, Tommy."

He can't stop. "We were going to call the police. But how could we? Dad's the policeman! Ha ha! He got called out to a car crash. I told Mom it would be real amazing if you were the one in the car crash." Tommy goes on breathlessly, imagining the scene. "There you are, dying on the side of the road. And your own father drives up in the patrol car to rescue you. Neat!"

"Be quiet, Tommy," Mom says as she comes back into the room. She washes my hand and puts a bandage on it. Then she takes a fresh cloth and gently wipes my cheek and the rest of my face. She says "tsk" again, bends down, and gives me a hug.

I'm speechless, but Tommy isn't. "Aren't you going to punish her, Mom?" he asks, pulling at Mom's skirt.

"Tommy, stop nattering and sit down. I'll warm you both up some hot chocolate. Maggie, go and change into your pyjamas. Your clothes are covered in dirt. You can tell us what happened when you come back."

oooooo

THE HOT CHOCOLATE tastes good. Mom's waiting for me to explain.

"I had to see Anna and give her something for her birthday. Riding my bike was the only way I could get to the farm."

Mom shakes her head. "You told me that you were going with Jerry to find more rocks for your report. When you didn't come home, I phoned his mother. She said Jerry had been home for hours. I spoke to Jerry, and he explained that he'd left you at the turnoff to the Lozowski place. You were coming home on your own."

"Don't be mad at Jerry, Mom."

"If I'm angry at anyone, it's you. I think you can imagine how worried I was when it got past seven-thirty and you weren't here. Dad was called out to an accident scene around four and I had no way to reach him. No way of knowing if you'd been one of the people involved in the accident."

"I'm sorry I worried you, Mom."

"You have no idea how upsetting it was to sit here waiting to hear from both you and your father." Her face is pale.

"I kept Mom company," Tommy says smugly.

Mom smiles. "He tried to cheer me up with knock-knock jokes!"

I smile back. "I bet that was a big help." I take a breath. "I'm really, really sorry. The afternoon went so quickly. I was playing with Bella and the girls, and then Anna said her dad was coming home and he'd give me a ride. But, Mom, it took ages for him to get home, and when he did, I didn't want to ride with him, so I started off by myself."

I pause to get my breath again. "Then a car came by with a man driving, and he wanted to give me a ride. I told him my father was in the RCMP, and he drove away. Then I saw some shadows in the field, but it was just cows. Then an animal, I think it was a coon, ran across the road. I fell off my bike. I looked for my glasses for ages. What am I going to do without them?"

I burst into tears. All the tension from the ride home in the dark pours onto my mother's shoulder. Her arms are tight around me. She's hugging me hard, and it feels good.

Mom's voice shakes. "I thought something terrible had happened to you, Maggie." She might have been crying. I can't tell. "I don't understand why you didn't tell us where you were going."

"Mom, you know you wouldn't have let me go. Not so far on my bike."

Mom sits back in the chair. "You're probably right." She pauses. "You're a good friend to Anna. I understand how much you wanted to see her."

"I'm glad I saw Bella and the girls too."

Mom looks at me. "But you'll have to be punished for what you've done. I'll talk it over with your father, but I think he'll agree that you'll be grounded from any bike rides with Jerry for a while."

I expected that.

Mom sighs. "We'll never find your glasses on that stretch of road. I'll have to order a new pair next week. You can wear your old ones to school."

Tommy pokes his head around the door. "I said you'd get it."

"Into bed *right now*, Tommy." Mom shoos him into his room.

When I'm in my room, she comes in and sits on the side of the bed.

"How are things with Anna's family?"

"Oh, Mom, Bella's already smiling and the girls are sweet, but it's too much work for Anna. She looks tired. I don't think she's done any school work. She could miss her grade seven year. She probably won't be in high school with me next year. It's not fair."

"My heart aches for that girl," Mom says. She strokes my hair and smiles. "You've had quite a day, and so have I. Go to sleep. I'll wait for your father to come in."

I catch her arm as she gets up. "Mom, please don't tell Dad how bad things are at the Lozowski farm. Anna's worried that the Welfare Department will take Bella away. Can the police do that?"

"Don't worry about it, Maggie. You've been a good friend to Anna. And in spite of the scare you've given me, I'm proud of you." She closes my door gently.

Mom said she's proud of me. She's never said that before. I pull the covers over my aching shoulders and sleep.

TUESDAY, MAY 25

TWO DAYS AGO I had a wonderful visit with Maggie but now I feel lonelier than I ever did. Papa arrived home yesterday and has finally started to fix the door on the outhouse. Mrs. Covey came over this afternoon, but when she saw Papa was home, she didn't stay long. The girls mope around all afternoon after she leaves.

"When's Maggie coming to play?" Helen asks for the second time today.

"Not for a while. It's hard for her to get out this far."

The girls still have terrible coughs and my throat is still sore. What happens if a baby as young as Bella gets a cold? Maybe pneumonia?

The boys are home from school and are outside helping Papa with the horses. It's time to start cooking hamburgers for supper. I light the kerosene lamp and sit the girls at the kitchen table with an old book they love. I put the hamburgers on to heat, get Bella's warm bottle, and pick her up from the cradle. She waves her arms in excitement when she sees the bottle.

"You're getting to be a big girl, aren't you?" I say. "Look at your chubby little arms."

Lucy's fussing at the table. She's been cranky all day. I lean over to give her a kiss on her cheek, but she pushes me away. My arm knocks against the lamp and tips it over. Kerosene sloshes onto the table. It bursts into flame and runs across the table like a river of fire, with pieces of the shattered glass chimney sticking up in the flames.

"Oh, Lucy, look what you've done!"

Quickly, I put Bella back into her cradle and grab a towel. I press on the flame, but I'm pressing on broken glass. The running flame threatens to fall off the table. I stop it by slamming my hand down hard. The flame is out, but there's a searing pain in my hand.

I take the burnt towel and throw it out the door and march back to Lucy. "Bad girl." Her little face looks up at me in shock.

I never talk to her like that.

I pick her up quickly. "I'm sorry, Lucy. I shouldn't have said that. It was an accident." I wipe away the yellow stream coming out of her nose. "I know you feel crabby today. I'm crabby too." My hand is throbbing.

I wet a cloth and press it between my hands. My heart pounds. The whole house could have caught on fire.

The door opens and Papa comes in. "What is wrong, Anna?"

"Everything's wrong," I wail. "It's all wrong since Mom died. I can't do anything right."

Papa looks at the broken glass sitting in kerosene on the table. He lifts the cloth I'm holding between my hands. "You are burned!"

"I burnt it putting out the fire. You need to pick up the glass, Papa."

"Damn. This is too hard for us," Papa says.

I start to moan from the fright and the pain. The girls huddle around, trying to comfort me, their faces crumpled with concern.

"Bad owie," Helen says. She soaks the cloth in more cold water and brings it over to me. It drips because she doesn't wring it out, but it helps cool the burn.

Bella starts to fuss for her bottle, and I push myself up to heat the milk again. Dad says, "Sit on the couch, Anna. I will get the baby's bottle."

"What about supper?"

"I do it."

Joe and Berny come in and help clean up the glass and kerosene. Joe brings Bella over to me along with the warm bottle and I sit up to feed her. Bella sucks hard at the milk, her bright eyes locked steadily into mine. She has no idea that we were all in danger. When she starts to feel full, she stops sucking, purses her lips, and smiles. I hold her tight against my face, and she rubs her little head from side to side, sliding on my wet cheek.

Papa brings a plate with my supper, but I can't eat. My hand is pulsing with pain. I rock Bella and watch the family around the supper table. Joe and Berny complain that the burgers are burnt. The girls pick at theirs. Papa sits, sullen, not talking to anyone.

Berny is putting the girls to bed and Bella is asleep in my arms when Papa comes and sits beside me on the couch. "It is too hard for you, Anna."

"I'm sorry, Papa. It hasn't been a good day." I try to reassure him. "I'll manage better tomorrow."

"I am not sure."

I'm not sure either. Today scared me. One of the girls could have been burned instead of me. The whole house could have caught on fire.

Papa goes to bed and I sit with Bella in the quiet house. I wonder if anyone in the family will remember that my birthday's coming up. I put Bella to bed and decide to open the present from Maggie. I unwrap it carefully and find a beautiful china bluebird perched on a wooden stand that says *The Bluebird of Hope.* I remember Maggie telling me her grandmother gave it to her. I can hardly believe Maggie's given it to me.

The Bluebird of Hope. Hope is what I need. Hope that I can take care of these three little girls who need me.

MONDAY, MAY 24

"YOUR MOTHER CALLED about you yesterday," Jerry says. "Were you okay?"

We're in the hall at the school lunch break. "Not really." I push the old glasses up on my nose. "I stayed until it was dark and fell on the way home. Now I'm grounded and can't go on bike rides for two weeks."

"Too bad," Tommy says. "Who says we can't still get together and do stuff? Want to come over to my place after school?"

"Sure." *That's new.*

At the lunchroom door, Jerry goes one way and I go another, to sit at the girls' table.

Carolyn smirks at me and chants, "Maggie and Jerry, sitting in a tree, K-I-S-S-I-N-G!" She laughs and twists around to see if the other girls will laugh with her. They do.

"Mind your own beeswax," I say to them, my cheeks burning.

oooooo

AFTER SCHOOL, I rush up the stairs to ask Mom if I can go over to Jerry's to finish some homework. "Okay," she says, "but leave your bike and walk over."

Mrs. Harvey gives us date squares she's just baked. She suggests we play Monopoly while she goes to the store. Neither of us feel like it, and Jerry says, "Let's practise with our yo-yos."

He teaches me Over the Moon, but his cute little black-and-white terrier keeps jumping up trying to catch the yo-yo. Jerry suggests we play phone tricks.

"I don't know what they are," I tell him.

"You find any old name in the book, and when the person answers you say funny things."

"Sounds neat."

Jerry goes first. He dials and says, "Hello. I hear you've got a hole in your roof."

I guess the person on the other end says, "Do I?"

Jerry says, "That explains why a drip like you is living there!"

He hangs up fast, and we can't stop laughing. I like his nerve.

"Your turn," he says. "You know Prince Albert tobacco that comes in a tin?"

"Yeah, sure. My parents have it."

Jerry says to find the number for Rickter's Grocery and tells me what to say.

When Mr. Rickter answers, I say, "Do you have Prince Albert in a can?"

He answers politely, "Yes, we do."

"Well, he's suffocating. You'd better let him out!" Then I hang up. We're laughing like crazy as Mrs. Harvey comes in the door.

When it's time to go, Jerry walks me to the barracks gate. "How about those cigarettes you were going to get?"

Why not? "Okay, come over tomorrow after school and I'll have them. I know where we can smoke them."

"Deal." He waves and heads out the gate.

oooooo

AT HOME, TOMMY and I are in the kitchen when Dad comes in. He and Mom stand talking with their backs to us. I cup my hand under my armpit and make a loud farting noise.

"Who did that?" Mom turns to glare at us.

"Shame, Tommy!" I say.

Dad grins at me. "You made that noise, didn't you, Mags?"

"I'm raising a couple of animals," Mom says. "Sit down. Dinner's ready."

I make my announcement as we start to eat. "I'm quitting the piano."

"You're what?" Mom says.

Dad looks as shocked as Mom. "Mags, you're doing so well. Wait till you get the results. You'll pass the exam with flying colours."

Mom takes a big breath. "Someday, Maggie, you'll be glad you can play. If you study for four or five more years you'll never be without an invitation to all the parties."

"Why would that be?" I cross my arms and glare at her.

"Because you'll be able to play the piano for kids to dance. You'll be the most popular girl there."

That's the dumbest reason I've ever heard, and I shout at Mom, "I don't want to be the person playing the piano. I want to be the one dancing!"

She pushes her chair back and gets up. "What next from you, Margaret Rose! *No,* you may not stop piano lessons. You can be so exasperating!" The lid slams on the bread tin, echoing along the kitchen counter and into my head.

I'm so furious that it's easy to steal the cigarettes. I watch until the coast is clear and grab two cigarettes from the tin on the shelf. Tommy's hanging around behind the door, but I don't think he sees me put them in my pocket. I stash them at the back of my bottom dresser drawer.

Before I go to bed, I go the kitchen to get a glass of water and hear Dad on the phone. He's saying Joseph Lozowski's name. I stop in the hall to listen, but Mom walks in.

"Off to bed. It's rude to listen to another person's phone call."

"What's Dad talking about? Has something happened to Anna or the baby?"

"None of your business, Maggie."

She hustles me off to my room. Dad's on the phone a long time.

I feel sick.

TUESDAY, MAY 25

EVEN THOUGH I'M tired, I try to be cheerful with the girls. If I didn't have all the work to do, I'd have more time to play with them.

Mama worked this hard every day. When I think back, I remember she wasn't always cheerful, but I never felt she was unhappy. I'm sure she got tired, but she was always so steady.

Of course, she didn't have school work to think about. Think about it is all I do. Every night, I plan to open a textbook when the girls are in bed, but then I have dishes to do and diapers to fold, and Bella to feed again. Tonight I think that maybe I could read when I'm feeding her, but when she fastens her bright eyes on me all I want to do is talk to her and tell her how beautiful she is.

She smiles all the time now. Every time I see that smile it trips a beat in my heart. My beautiful baby. Mama's gift to me. I settle Bella's warm body against my shoulder, brushing my cheek against hers, and sing softly to her. The burn on my palm is red and sore.

Maggie

TUESDAY, MAY 25

AFTER SCHOOL, I get the cigarettes from where I've stashed them in my room and go out to the backyard. I pass May, who's standing by the back door of the office getting some fresh air.

"Hi, May," I call as I open the gate to the lane.

Jerry's there already.

"Got them," I say, and we're both grinning.

I lead him to a place under the overhanging roof behind the garage. "We can smoke here without anyone seeing us," I tell him.

We sit with our backs against the garage wall, and I take the cigarettes out of my pocket. "Sorry they're a bit bent."

I hand one to Jerry, who strikes a match, and we light up.

It's sure easier than smoking a dried weed. You draw in once and it's going. Almost too easy. I can't take long puffs the way Mom and Dad do, because the smoke stings my nose. I make a circle with my mouth and exhale in a long breath, just like women do in the movies.

Jerry tilts his head and looks at me through narrowed eyes. "This is the life," he sighs.

The hair falling over his forehead adds to his tough stance. I try tilting my head and squinting the way he does, but it makes me feel a bit dizzy.

I hear someone walking past the garage.

"Quick, put it out, Jerry," I whisper, and we stub our cigarettes in the dirt. They're smoked less than halfway. The footsteps go past, and I peek around the corner of the garage.

"The coast is clear."

"Close call," Jerry says. "Guess I'd better go home."

We try to act normally as we stroll to the back gate. Jerry leaves and I go upstairs. Luckily, no one sees me. I brush my teeth in the bathroom, then lie on my bed and try to read. My stomach feels weird, but I'm definitely not sorry I smoked my first real cigarette. Smoking definitely makes you feel mature.

Then a feeling of doom comes over me. The feeling you get when you know you've done something wrong and you're waiting to see if anything will happen. I decide to rearrange the things on my dresser. One by one, I move the pieces of the brush and comb dresser set I got last Christmas. I straighten the photograph of Dad. I study my face in the mirror, thinking that without glasses, my eyes are actually more violet than blue.

Suddenly Mom's angry face looms in the mirror behind me. "Into the kitchen ... *now.*"

I know I'm going to get it. I put my glasses back on and go as slowly as I can down the hall. Mom and Dad are sitting at the kitchen table. I stand in the doorway.

"Get in here, Maggie," Dad says in his stern police voice.

I come closer, but they don't suggest I sit.

Dad starts. "We know you've been smoking with Jerry. I can't believe you'd do such a thing."

Mom's voice is strained. "What ever gave you the idea that it's all right for a girl your age to smoke?"

I stare right at her. "I've been watching you puff away since the day I was born." Mom snaps her head back as though I've slapped her.

"Adults can smoke. Children can't. Where did you get the cigarettes?" Dad asks.

"Over there," I say, pointing to the shelf.

"So, you stole them from us?" His mouth is a grimace, not like my dad at all.

"I guess so."

That does it for Mom. "She *guesses* so!"

"Tommy told you, didn't he?" I yell.

"Never mind who told us," Dad says. "Our problem is how we're going to teach you a lesson so you never do this again. You're almost thirteen. We expect you to know enough not to steal and not to smoke."

I take a deep breath. It's impossible to explain why I do things. I don't understand them myself.

Dad takes me by the arm, leads me into the living room, and tells me to sit on the chesterfield. "If smoking is what you want to do, then let's see you with a real smoke. We'll see how you handle it."

Dad goes to his desk and takes out a box of cigars from the middle drawer. I've only ever seen him smoke a cigar once. I remember I liked the smell of it.

"Here, have one," he says, tossing a fat brown cigar at me. He flicks a lighter and puts it to the cigar. "Now, start smoking that."

The cigar is huge in my mouth, but I intend to show him I can smoke it. I take a puff. You have to pull harder on a cigar. I blow out grey smoke toward Dad, who's standing in front of me. I take another couple of puffs, lean back, cross my legs, and wave the cigar in the air. I'm trying to act sophisticated. Then I realize I don't want to smoke it any more. I hold it out to Dad.

He has a funny look on his face. "That's not enough. Have some more."

I put my mouth around the cigar and draw in, but this time, it doesn't feel good at all. I try to hand the cigar back to Dad.

He shakes his head. "Don't stop now. You like smoking so much, let's see you keep going."

Through the cloud of smoke around me I see Tommy peering in from the doorway, his eyes wide. I take another puff, but this time it's too much and I know I'm going to throw up. I stub the cigar in the ashtray. "I'm going to my room now, Dad."

"Hope you enjoyed the cigar, Maggie," he says, looking at me steadily.

"It was different," I say as I get up out of the chair. He's not going to know how sick I feel. I saunter out of the room, my head spinning, and nearly fall over Tommy in the doorway.

"Get out of my way, you squealer," I croak as I smack him across the chest and rush to the bathroom—where I throw up.

Anna

THURSDAY, MAY 27

PAPA REMEMBERED MY birthday today and everyone sang "Happy Birthday" at the breakfast table, the little girls singing their hearts out.

"My kid sister is a teenager!" Joe said. "Hard to believe."

"You're the best," Berny says, giving me a punch in the arm.

After the boys have left for school and the girls are playing in the living room, Dad calls me over to the kitchen table. "Anna, a woman from the Welfare Department is coming. Ten o'clock this morning."

"Why? What does she want?" My heart is thundering.

He takes a long breath. "Lucy and Helen will live in town with a foster mother."

I can't believe I've heard right. "What do you mean? What does foster mean? Someone's taking the girls away?"

Dad can't look at me. "It is for the best, Anna. I have decided. The woman from Welfare helped. You must pack the girls' clothes."

I feel as though I've been hit over the head. "What do you mean you have decided? No one asked me. I won't let anyone take my sisters away."

"It is done, Anna. Bring down the clothes."

"I won't do it." I go over and sit by the girls. They look scared.

Papa pulls me to my feet. "Upstairs now, Anna. You stay here, girls."

I turn to go and yell, "Mama would hate you for this! I hate you for this!"

My body feels numb and my legs move mechanically as I climb the stairs to the girls' bedroom. We don't own a suitcase, so I get a cardboard box and put the few clothes they have in the box, the dirty clothes mixed in with the clean. I put in a hairbrush and sweaters and a rag doll the girls play with. They make a pathetic pile in the bottom of the cardboard box. I hear someone at the outside door and go slowly down the stairs, carrying the half-empty box.

A dumpy woman in a grey coat is talking to Helen and Lucy. They stare at her.

"You'll have a car ride to your new home in town," I hear the woman say. "You'll like Mrs. Brooks. She has a new doll for each of you."

The girls turn to look at me, and I can see they're torn. They're confused about what's happening, but I can see they're also excited at the thought of new dolls.

Helen asks, "Can we take our blocks with us?"

"I guess so," I say. I try not to let them see how upset I am. Helen and I gather the blocks and put them on top of the clothes.

I pass the cardboard box to the woman, who smiles at me. "Anna, your father told me you've done a good job keeping the family together these past weeks. This new arrangement will be for the best for your sisters. Mrs. Brooks loves children. She's one of our best foster mothers."

"We love children here too," I say, looking right at her.

"I know that, Anna. Mrs. Brooks asked me to tell you that you'll always be welcome in her home. You can visit whenever you like. You won't lose touch with the girls."

I hear the words, but I can't believe the enormity of what's happening. And it's happening today. My birthday! The woman's firm manner tells me Helen and Lucy will be leaving the house with her.

She takes Helen's hand and leads her out to the car. Papa picks Lucy up and puts her in the back seat beside Helen. The Welfare woman is about to shut the car door.

"NO!" I say loudly. They all stare at me.

This is my chance to stop her. But how can I? If I drag the girls out of the car, I'll upset them. Papa will just put them back.

"Wait!" I call, leaning into the back seat. "I want a big hug from both of you."

"Love you, Anna," Helen says, and Lucy leans over to plant a wet kiss on my cheek.

"Be good girls," I say, choking on the words.

oooooo

PAPA PUTS HIS arm around my shoulder as we watch the car turn onto the road, taking my little sisters away. I shake him off and go back into the house, where Bella has started to cry. I go upstairs to change her and then bring her down. Dad's outside chopping wood.

Bella and I wander around the house. It feels like an empty barn. No little girls running around, no little voices calling me. I look at their hand-me-down boots by the door. I forgot to put them in the box. A dim light from the window falls in an empty square on the rug where my sisters had been sitting with their blocks.

The girls were taken away so quickly. They went so easily. They were so good, doing what they were told. They even smiled at me from the back seat of the car. But they are *my* sisters and I *was* looking after them. Lucy's just learning to talk and Helen's so smart with all her questions.

I realize I'm holding Bella too tightly as I walk around. She wants to wiggle and kick, so I put her on the blanket on the floor while I wash the breakfast dishes and heat soup for lunch.

Papa comes back in and sits at the table watching Bella doing her air crawl, flailing her arms and legs like a windmill.

I put two bowls of soup on the table and sit down beside him. "How could you do this? How could you let that woman take the girls away?"

"I ask the Welfare people to do it, Anna."

"Why, Papa? It wasn't too hard for me."

Then I remember crying the other day when I burned my hand. Crying and saying everything was wrong.

"It's my fault, isn't it? I was exhausted that day. The day I hurt my hand. I didn't mean I couldn't take care of them. It's because I complained that day, isn't it?"

"It is not, Anna. I could not let you go on. You are too young."

"I didn't want you to take them away."

"It was my decision." Papa pours himself another cup of coffee and sits back down. He seems nervous. I wonder why he's not going outside. I pick Bella up and rock her.

I'm staring out the window when another car drives up. A man and a woman get out and come to our door. I think they must have turned off the main road and are lost. At the knock, Papa jumps up and goes to let them in. He invites them to sit on the sofa, and I notice the woman is staring at Bella.

Papa turns to me. "The Woodmans will take Bella to their home in the United States."

"Oh no! They can't!" I hold Bella tighter. "They can't take our baby!"

"It is for the best, Anna. We have to let her go."

The woman pulls a pink baby sweater and bonnet out of her bag and hands it to me. "I knitted these for Bella," she says. "Why not try them on her?"

I have the wild thought of clutching Bella and running out the door. I could run along the creek and out to the main road. But then where? Where could I take her? A girl and a baby. There's no place for us to go. Papa would come and get me. I'm not strong enough to fight him.

My hands shake as I put the sweater and bonnet on Bella and tie the ribbons under her dimpled chin. Both the man and the woman are watching with wide smiles. The woman leans over and says, "Hello, little girl."

Bella smiles back at the woman.

I can't stand it.

"Pack Bella's things, Anna," Papa says.

"You can't make me do that!" I yell.

I rush up to Papa and scream in his face, "Don't let them take Bella away. Mama wouldn't want it."

A storm is raging in my head. I turn to the woman. "Don't do this to our family. I hate you for coming here. You are *not* taking our baby. I won't let you. Go away!"

The woman and her husband stop smiling and look at Papa.

"It is decided, Anna," he says. "I have signed papers."

He grips my arm and leads me to the stairs. "Get Bella's things *now*."

I shake him off and pick Bella up. I rush up the stairs, almost tripping. I put her down on the bed. How can I fight my father? I start putting Bella's few clothes in a cloth bag. I look over at her every minute. She's waving her arms and blowing little bubbles out of her mouth. She looks adorable in the pink sweater.

As I come down the stairs, I keep kissing Bella's face. Papa tries to lift her out of my arms. I hold tighter. "Please, please, Papa, don't do this. You can't give Bella away. I beg you with all my heart not to do this."

"Quiet, Anna." Papa pries Bella out of my arms. He passes her to the woman. The couple turn and start to walk out the door, the woman carrying Bella. My father just stands there.

I reach up and pound him on the chest with both fists. "Stop them, Papa. Stop them! You can't let them do this."

He grabs my hands and holds them in his. "Do not hit me, Anna."

I stand there helplessly as the man and woman get in the car. The doors close and the car drives away, taking Bella with them. I stare at the empty road.

Papa turns me back into the house. He pushes me into a chair at the kitchen table. I'm breathing hard.

"It is for the best, Anna."

"I can't let her go! Bella's so little!" I scream into my father's face. "I can't believe you'd let strangers take our baby away. You're making me break the promise I made to my mother."

"It is done, Anna."

The look on his face tells me it's too late. I've lost. I put my head on my arms and sob until my whole body hurts. I lift my head, and he's still sitting across from me. There are tears in his eyes.

I glare at him. "This is the worst thing you could ever do to me. It's my birthday, and my life is over."

"Listen to me, Anna. I could not let you go on. You wear yourself out. You need school. To have life with people your own age. And you can see Helen and Lucy when you're in town."

"But I've lost Bella . . ." I wail.

Papa sighs. "It is done, Anna." He goes outside, shutting the door behind him.

I hurl myself face down on the couch. I'm in a place I've never been before. My whole body is shaking. The terrible wailing sounds are coming from me.

When the boys come in from school, they rush over to me. Papa has met them, and they know their sisters have been taken away.

"Oh, Anna. I can't believe it," Berny says, sitting down beside me.

Joe says, "It had to happen, Anna. There was too much work for you to manage. We could all see that."

"Then why didn't you help me? Now I've broken my promise to Mama!" I yell at him.

I run upstairs to be alone, where no one can try to comfort me. There will be no happiness in my life after this. I will never forget this birthday to my dying day. If I can't have the girls, I don't want to live.

Maggie

SATURDAY, MAY 29

IT'S SATURDAY, and Dad calls me to the phone. Since the smoking disaster, he's stopped calling me Mags.

To my surprise, it's Anna calling from the pay phone downtown. She's in Deep Creek with her father and wants us to meet at the school yard.

I run all the way there. I'm gasping for breath when I reach her. She's sitting on the steps of the deserted school. I wipe my steamed-up glasses on the leg of my shorts and plop myself down beside her.

Then I realize Anna's crying hard.

"Anna, what's wrong?"

She has her hands over her face, and tears run out between her fingers. It's something terrible.

When she can finally talk, her words come slowly. "Two days ago, on my birthday... a woman came from the Welfare Department . . . she took Lucy and Helen away."

Anna stops to take a breath. "She marched into the house . . . just took the girls away. I didn't even get to brush their hair."

I'm horrified. It was my father who made this happen. I heard him talking about Mr. Lozowski on the phone. He was making arrangements for this.

"Anna, I'm so sorry."

"Then something worse happened." She wipes her wet hands on her slacks.

What could be worse?

"Right after that, a man and his wife drove up in their car . . . They took Bella away! Papa made me pack up her things." Her sobs echo against the brick wall and over the empty playground.

"Oh no! They can't do that." I feel cold all over.

Anna takes big gulps of air. "That's what I said to Papa . . . He said it was for the best. He said I wasn't managing."

She shakes her head. "I *was* managing, Maggie. I was tired one day and complained to him. It's my own fault."

But I know it was *my* father's fault. That's something Anna must never find out.

Anna lifts her head, a defeated look on her face that's all puffy from crying. "They made me break my promise to my mother."

"I know. I'm so sorry."

"Dad told me I can visit Helen and Lucy in town. He says I can go back to school too."

"Isn't that a good thing?"

"I'm too unhappy to think about going back to school."

"What about Bella? Will you be able to visit her?"

"No, that's the worst thing. The people who adopted her live in the United States. It's a huge country. I'll *never* see Bella again." Anna catches her breath and wipes her streaming wet face. "She was doing so well. You remember her great smiles. She smiled so early."

"The people who took her, what were they like?"

"The woman spoke to Bella in a quiet voice. The man didn't take his eyes off her. Dad says they had a baby girl who died before she was a year old. They were in Canada trying to find a baby."

Anna slumps against me. She hasn't mentioned my father. She can *never* know he's responsible for this terrible thing. I'll have to keep this huge secret to myself for the rest of my life.

I put my arm around her. "You'll be able to come into town so we can get together, won't you?"

"Yes, when I get the chores done."

"Come to my place whenever you can."

Anna brightens a little. "Miss Alexander came out to the farm yesterday. She knew about the girls being taken away.

If I work hard in the next month, she says I'll go into high school with you and the rest of the class."

"I'll help you. It'll be easy for us. And you're a whiz at arithmetic."

She tries to smile, but it's a weak smile that doesn't make her look happy. I walk with Anna to the service station on Front Street, where she's arranged to meet her father. When we say goodbye, I wonder if I'll ever hear her laugh again. But how can *I* ever laugh again with a Judas for a father?

I run back home, rush up the front stairs into the RCMP office, past a startled May, and stop in front of my father's big desk.

Dad looks up from his papers and raises his eyebrows. I don't give him a chance to speak.

"I never knew my father was a traitor!" I shout.

"Calm down and sit," Dad says firmly.

I stay standing and glare at him."Why did you have Anna's sisters taken away?" I glare at him.

Dad takes a deep breath and leans across the desk toward me. "Maggie, I did what a police officer has to do when someone makes a complaint. Mrs. Covey spoke to me about her concerns for Anna's family. My job was to talk to Mr. Lozowski. When I did, he told me things were too difficult for Anna."

"He could have stayed home and helped her!"

"No, he's a farmer. He has to take care of his cattle and work in the fields. Anyway, he'd been to the Welfare Department to ask for help before I talked to him."

I plunk down on the chair across from the desk. "You mean he'd already decided to have the girls taken away? You weren't the one who made him do it?"

"No, I wasn't. I don't have the power to do that."

"But Anna's lost all her sisters!"

"Think about it. It's for the best. It was impossible for the family to continue the way it was. Anna's father knew it. Someday Anna will understand that her father was trying to make sure his girls have a good future. That includes Anna."

"But Anna's life is ruined."

Dad shakes his head. "No, it's not. She has a chance to go to school and live her own life now."

"You don't understand. How can Anna ever be happy when she's broken her promise to her mother?"

"The baby will be cared for by her new parents. By letting Bella go, Anna *is* keeping the promise to her mother. Anna's given that baby a future. Can you understand that?"

I pick at my thumbnail. "Sort of. But what's Bella's future without her own family?"

"I was told Bella's with good people." Dad rubs the back of his neck. "The adults have worked things out, Maggie."

"Sometimes kids know what's best for other kids."

"Adults have the experience to make the right decisions, Maggie," Dad says. "You should know that Anna's father is trying to straighten out his own life. The plan is for the two little girls to be back with the family in a few years when they're older. It's a good plan."

I'm not so sure about that, I think as I walk back down the office stairs. My father didn't see Anna's face when I said goodbye to her.

Anna

FRIDAY, JUNE 4

IT'S STRANGE TO be back at school, but I'm trying hard to catch up with the work I missed. Miss Alexander is helping me, and so are Maggie and Jerry. Maggie told me she got a B on the project—she had to finish it by herself. She also told me that bison is the correct species name, but buffalo is commonly used here on the prairies.

At recess, Maggie and Jerry are laughing about something over at the art table when Carolyn comes up to me.

"I guess you notice that things have changed since you've been away. Maggie is best friends with Jerry now. Boy crazy, I'd say."

I'm too surprised to say anything. I shrug my shoulders and turn away. Maybe that's true. Maybe Maggie and I aren't best friends any more. I put my head down to finish the science assignment. It still hurts to hold a pencil in the hand that was burned.

I look up to see Maggie standing by my desk. "Let's eat lunch in our special place today."

"Sure," I say. Does she plan to tell me we aren't best friends anymore?

We sit by ourselves outside on the bench. Right away, Maggie starts complaining about her mother.

"Mom's so mean. She won't let me quit music lessons and she lets Tommy get away with murder."

"Tommy's just five years old, Maggie."

"Well, the only time my mother was nice to me was when I fell off my bike. I should arrange to fall off every day."

I know she's trying to be funny, and I guess I should be glad that she can talk to me about this. But I've heard it all before. It frustrates me when she never does anything about it.

"Did you ever come straight out and ask your parents if you're adopted?"

"It's never the right time."

Somehow it's always the right time to complain to me.

"Just *do* it, Maggie!" I tell her.

"Easy for you to say. You don't have to live with my mother."

"Stop whining! At least you have a mother."

Maggie stares at me, and my words hang in the air between us. She gets up from where we're sitting and walks into the school, leaving me alone on the bench.

The afternoon drags as I try to catch up on school work. The room smells of glue from the art table and wet jackets in the cloakroom. As soon as school's out I'll find Maggie and tell her I'm sorry. But when the bell rings, she grabs her jacket and dashes out the door. I rush after her, but I can't find her. So I leave.

Today is the first visit with my sisters. I walk along the streets to where Mrs. Brooks lives, hoping I might see Maggie, but I know I won't. The barracks is in the other direction.

Mrs. Brooks opens the door with a big smile, and the girls rush up behind her, reaching to kiss me.

"Come see our pussy cat," Helen says.

Lucy grabs a grey kitten in the living room. She squishes the cat in her arms and holds him up to me.

"Mrs. B got a kitten especially for us. We call him Boo!" Helen says.

"But that's what we call our cat on the farm," I say, trying not to feel hurt.

"We know that," Helen says. "We like the name."

"It was kind of Mrs. Brooks to get a kitten for you."

"I can count to twenty, Anna."

"Can you? Good girl, Helen."

The girls are wearing matching red plaid dresses tied with a sash at the back. Nothing our family could ever afford.

"You look pretty in your new dresses," I tell them.

Helen twirls around and Lucy lifts up her dress to show me she's wearing underpants. "Look. Pants!"

Mrs. Brooks smiles. "You did a good job of getting her toilet trained, Anna. She's a big girl now, aren't you, Lucy?"

"Um, yep," Lucy says.

"Come see our room," Helen says, taking me by the hand. Lucy follows behind. The twin beds with pink bedspreads look as though they belong in a magazine.

"And look at our dolls." Helen holds up a golden-haired doll with blue eyes and a pretty face.

"Mine," Lucy says, holding up a doll that's almost as big as she is.

We play with the dolls for a while. They have so many doll outfits, including coats, hats, and fur muffs. I used to wish for a doll with clothes like this.

Mrs. Brooks comes into the room and suggests I might like to take the girls for a walk. "Why not go to the library, Anna? I want Helen and Lucy get new books every week."

I dress the girls in their new sweaters, so much nicer than the worn ones they had at home.

While we're walking, Helen says, "She told us to call her Mrs. B."

"Misbee," Lucy says proudly.

"Do you like her?" I ask.

"She's nice to us and we have pretty things," Helen says, "but we miss you, Anna."

"I miss you too," I say. I squeeze my eyes to keep the tears inside as we walk along the sidewalk.

Their life here is better than I could ever give them. Warm sweaters. Library books. And Mrs. Brooks is better with them than I was. Lucy is talking more and she's out of diapers. New dresses and new boots. They've got everything little girls could want.

On the way back, the girls skip along the street with their picture books. They even know where to go.

Helen says, "Papa came to see us this morning. He brought candy."

Lucy smacks her lips. "Hum, jellies."

When we're back in their bedroom, I see two flannel nightgowns hanging on the back of the door. I used to love it when the girls crawled into my bed, their warm little bodies curled up beside me. It hurts so much to know that they're curling up beside someone else.

When I say goodbye, we can't stop hugging each other.

Papa is waiting for me at the service station. He looks better. He shaves every day now and he's been to the barber to get his hair cut.

"You look good, Papa," I say.

"Five days now I stop drinking."

"That's really good, Papa." I cross my fingers that he can keep it up.

Papa starts the truck and turns onto the highway. "The girls are well, Anna."

"It doesn't mean I don't miss them, Papa."

On the way home, I keep thinking about how Maggie looked at me when I said that mean thing. Carolyn was right. I don't blame Maggie for preferring Jerry's company. I've become a miserable person.

Papa stops the truck by our house and I sit in the front seat looking out at the farm. Nothing has changed. The paint on the house is still peeling. The grey barn with one side collapsing is still here. The three horses stand in their favourite corner of the field, the wind flipping their tails in the air.

But my whole world has changed. No grey diapers hanging on the line. No little girls' voices calling to me.

And an empty space inside me where sweet Bella was.

Maggie

SUNDAY, JUNE 6

I'M LYING ON my bed thinking about how mean Anna was to me. It felt like being slapped when she said I was whining about my mother. It was a cruel thing to say. Who can you talk to about things if not your best friend?

Maybe she's changed since all her sisters were taken away. I feel sorry for her, but she turned on me. Friends shouldn't do that. I decide that from now on, Anna can say what she likes, but I won't let it hurt me.

Tommy wanders into the bedroom. "Mom and Dad sent me out of the kitchen. They're talking about you again."

He's quiet, just standing there, then he blurts out, "Are you mad at me, Maggie?"

"Yes, I am. You're a dirty squealer, telling Mom and Dad about me smoking."

"I didn't! It was May. I heard her telling Dad." His face is crumbling. "I didn't snitch on you, Maggie. Honest."

It *could* have been May. She saw me going behind the garage with Jerry. I guess I was wrong. "Okay, Tommy. Sorry. But try not to be such a brat all the time."

In a flash, that smile comes out. The smile that goes from one side of his face to the other. He's not a bad kid. If he ends up stealing and smoking it will be because of me.

Oh, Gram, did you watch me steal the cigarettes? Are you close by? Are you disappointed because I'm behaving badly?

I hear Mom calling me to the kitchen. What have I done now? I walk slowly down the hall, fearing the worst.

Mum's wearing her apron and holding one out for me. "It's time you learned how to make pastry."

I'm surprised. Mom's not mad. She's never asked me to bake with her before.

"What about Tommy? You're always saying I should include him."

She's getting out the mixing bowl. "You know Tommy. He'd have flour all over the floor."

I can't believe it. She never says anything bad about Tommy.

"Wash your hands and bring me the flour from the cupboard."

Mom shows me how to crumble the lump of hard lard into the flour and then roll out the pastry. I fill the base with preserved Saskatoon berries, sugar, and lemon juice, then Mom shows me how to make a professional-looking pattern around the edge. She makes three slits in the top and puts the pie in the oven.

She gets us each a glass of lemonade and we sit together at the kitchen table. This is the first time I've been across the table from Mom with no one else around. No Tommy to demand her attention. No Dad who gets mine.

It's my chance to ask if I'm adopted. Just do it, Anna told me. Just *do* it.

The house is quiet except for the ticking of the kitchen clock.

Of course, Mom could deny that I'm adopted.

She could get mad.

She could start to cry.

Or I could fall down in a faint.

I shuffle my feet back and forth on the floor. Just *do* it.

"Mom, can I ask you something?"

"Sure." She sits back in her chair.

"I was wondering if I . . . if I'm . . . I know this sounds silly." My heart is thudding like a truck engine. "I was wondering if I was adopted."

"Why would you think that, Maggie?" Mom sits up and looks hard at me.

"I don't know. I guess because you seem to like Tommy better than me. It's because he can do no wrong and everything I do is wrong. It makes me think you don't love me."

There. It's out.

Mom reaches across the table and takes my hand. "Well, I do love you. And you are certainly not adopted, Maggie. I'd better show you something."

While Mom goes into the bedroom, I wait at the table, hardly daring to breathe. She comes back with an official birth certificate. I see the date and my name. Mom's name is there and Dad's too. I weighed seven pounds two ounces and was born in Regina. I stare at the paper.

Mom gets an old photograph album from the bookcase and flips through the pages. She stops at a photograph of a young woman in a loose smock standing beside Dad in front of a house. It's Mom, and she's obviously expecting. Dad is beaming. I run my finger over the picture. That's me under the smock.

Mom says, "You're smiling. Do you feel better now?"

"I do, Mom. I'm glad you showed me."

I feel a whole lot better. "I just needed to know for sure, Mom." I can't stop smiling.

"How did you get the idea you were adopted?"

I take a deep breath. "Because sometimes you're mean to me."

Mom is quiet and shakes her head.

Have I gone too far?

She looks right at me. "I know I'm strict with you, Maggie. I think it's because you remind me so much of myself. We're both strong-willed. I remember what it was like growing up, and I don't want you to make any mistakes. I want you to be the best you can be."

Her eyes are watery. "It frightened me that night you came home so late from Anna's farm. You could have been badly hurt. I saw how vulnerable you are and I wanted to feel close to you. That's why I wanted us to bake together today."

I think there are tears in my own eyes.

"Mom, I'm sorry I've been acting crummy lately. Like stealing the cigarettes and snapping back at you."

"Yes, those were mistakes, but you're also a very caring girl. I've seen how loving you were to your grandmother and how loyal you are to Anna."

Mom touches my arm. "We're so much alike. I know I'm quick-tempered at times, but, Maggie, so are you! There should never be any doubt in your mind that you're my daughter."

She's right. Tommy's not like us at all.

Mom takes my hand. "Let's both try to watch our tempers. We can do better." Her blue eyes sparkle as she smiles at me, and I think how pretty she is. In lots of ways she's the perfect wife for Dad.

The bell on the stove rings and we take the pie out. Dark purple juice has bubbled through the slits and spread over the top of the pie. Mom nods toward the pie, and I nod back.

"Why not?" she says, putting out two plates.

I get forks, and we sit at the table and cut two pieces. It's delicious.

"You'll be a good cook, Maggie."

"Take after my mother," I say, and we both grin.

It's a fresh start for me with Mom.

I think of Anna without a mother to help her figure things out. "I'm lucky to have you, Mom," I say quietly. She pats my arm, then stands to take our plates to the sink.

"Come and help me clean up," she says.

WEDNESDAY, JUNE 9

LAST NIGHT I was doing my homework at the kitchen table and I heard Bella cry. It was her special "I'm hungry" cry. I was almost at the top of the stairs before I remembered Bella wasn't there.

I came down, put my head on the kitchen table, and let my tears out. One thing I've learned is that there are always more tears to come. There's a bottomless well of sadness inside me. A well that will never empty.

Maggie

SATURDAY, JUNE 12

JERRY PHONED THIS afternoon to see if he could come over to play catch with Tommy. He says he'll bring his dog. Tommy bounces around with excitement when I tell him.

"I really love dogs, Jerry," Tommy says when we meet Jerry in the front yard of the barracks. "What's his name?"

"Wellington."

Tommy looks at Jerry with a rapt expression on his face. "Why did you call him that?"

"I dunno," Jerry says. "He's my dog, so I got to pick. I like the name Wellington."

"Neat," Tommy says.

I cringe when I notice Tommy still has a red mark on his forehead.

Tommy chases the dog, who runs around in circles, then he stops, breathless, and comes back to play catch with us.

He grins at us. "If I had a dog I'd name him after my favourite cartoon character."

"Who's your favourite cartoon character?" Jerry and I ask at the same time.

"Mickey Mouse."

Jerry and I exchange a look. Tommy doesn't see Jerry's eyes crinkling at the corners. We both think it's hilarious that Jimmy wants to name his dog after a Walt Disney mouse.

Tommy's too excited to notice that we're laughing at him. He picks Wellington up, squeezing him so hard the dog jumps down from his arms and runs away.

"Hey, Jerry," Tommy says. "I got a good joke."

"Let's hear it."

"It's a dirty joke about a horse."

Tommy looks over at me. "You're kidding?"

"Nope. It's a *real* dirty joke. You sure you want to hear it?"

"Just tell the joke, Tommy," I say.

"Here's the dirty joke. Ready?"

"We're ready."

"A white horse fell in the mud. Ha ha!"

Jerry gives Tommy a punch on the shoulder.

"I got another one," Jimmy says.

"No, Tommy!" I say.

"Knock-knock."

"Don't answer," I tell Jerry. "It'll be an old joke."

Jerry smiles and says, "Who's there?"

"Ignore him," I say.

"Shut up, Maggie," Tommy says to me.

"Shut up Maggie who?" says Jerry.

"Do it *right*!" Tommy stamps his foot. "Police," he says to Jerry.

"Okay. Police who?"

Big smile. "Pu-lease let me in. It's cold out here!"

Tommy's chuckling at his own joke. I don't often see him having this kind of fun. When Mom calls him he looks disappointed, but he punches Jerry on the arm and runs up the stairs.

Jerry and I sit on the ledge beside the garage. "Tommy's a great kid. Fun to have around," he says.

"I guess he's okay. For a five-year-old."

"Way to go, Princess Maggie," Jerry grins, then looks serious. "I notice you and Anna aren't so friendly anymore. What's up?"

I didn't think anyone had noticed. Anna and I haven't spoken for more than a week. "I think she's changed. She's critical of me lately."

"That doesn't sound like Anna."

"I don't want to talk about it."

As Jerry's leaving, Dad comes around the corner of the building. He's been on patrol and he's wearing his scarlet tunic and leather boots, which make him look very tall and official. Jerry catches his breath as Dad strides up with his hand out.

"You must be Jerry." His deep voice is familiar to me, but not to Jerry.

"Yes, sir. Jerry Harvey. I live with my mother over at 2657 Alder."

"I don't need your address and there's no need to call me sir," Dad says. "You can call me Sergeant Neilson. I hear you and Maggie have been up to some adventures."

"Well, yes, sir. I guess you could say that." Jerry's eyes are fixed on the holster at Dad's belt. Is he remembering what it was like in the cells? Or is he like me and always sure he's guilty of something, but never exactly sure what? Poor Jerry.

Dad grins. "How about coming over for a cigar one day?"

"No thanks, sir." Jerry shakes his head, not looking my dad in the eye. I think Jerry's hands are trembling.

"Well, if you don't want to smoke, come on over on the weekend and I'll give you a ride in the patrol car."

"That would be great, sir," Jerry says, taking deep breaths and heading for the gate.

"No need to call me sir," Dad calls back as we turn toward the stairs to our place.

oooooo

I FEEL PLEASED about the day. Tommy's sitting on the floor, pushing around his collection of cars. He won't learn to read until next year, and I remember Gram saying I had an expressive voice. I ask Tommy if he'd like me to read to him when he goes to bed.

"Oh, man! You bet." He runs to get into his pyjamas.

I climb up beside him in his bed and open a book called *Little Tim and the Brave Sea Captain.*

"You'll like this one. It's about a boy who has adventures at sea."

Tommy slides his hot body up against me. I'm aware of his even breaths as I read. After a while he pokes my arm. "Hey, Maggie."

"What?"

"Hope you know that I'm yours until Niagara Falls! Get it?"

"For heaven's sake, Tommy. If you want me to keep reading, you'd better stop cracking jokes."

When I come out of Tommy's bedroom, Dad's reading in the living room. I go over and sit down beside him, close enough to smell his aftershave. Old Spice. It's in the bottle with a blue sailing ship on the bathroom shelf.

"What are you reading?" I ask.

"This is a novel about some prisoners in the last war who attempted a bold escape from a German prison camp."

"Did they get out?"

"A few of them did, but most didn't."

"What about that prisoner we had here, Dad? Will he ever be let out of the mental institution?"

"Maybe. If they feel he's better."

"I still have a hard time understanding how he could feel two things at the same time. Wanting to kill his wife and baby and then feeling bad about it."

"We can all feel two things at the same time. I can be disappointed in you and still love you."

"*Are* you disappointed in me?"

"Well, I'm not sure I can trust you now. It's hard for a policeman to feel proud of a daughter who steals."

How terrible! My own father doesn't trust me. He doesn't feel proud of me. I want to turn my life back to the day before I stole the cigarettes.

Dad picks up his book. "Good night now."

This is the worst thing that could happen. I knew something was wrong when he stopped calling me Mags. I've totally wrecked the special thing we had between us. He's not even proud of me. I might as well be dead.

SUNDAY, JUNE 13

I DESPERATELY NEED to talk to Maggie. I hurt her feelings. I could see by her face when I told her she should be grateful she had a mother. She needed me to listen and I was impatient. I got tired of her always talking about being adopted and never asking her mother. I accused her of whining. You can't take back a word like that.

Papa's brought me into town this morning to visit with the girls, but I told him I need to talk to Maggie first. Maybe she won't even want to see me.

There's a telephone outside the pharmacy. I put in a nickel and dial her number. Maggie answers.

"Hi," I say. "It's Anna."

"I know it's you, Anna."

"Can I come over?"

It seems to me there's a pause before she says, "Ring the bell at the top of the stairs."

I walk up the hill to the RCMP barracks. The stairs up to her apartment are steep. It would be easy to turn back, but I force myself to the top. I have to try to make things right. Maggie opens the door on the first ring. She introduces to me her mother, who's busy in the kitchen. They have a stove that's electric and a real refrigerator, not an ice box. Her mother seems friendly, but Maggie's right. They don't look much alike.

Maggie takes me to her bedroom and shuts the door. We sit on her bed.

I take a breath. "I came over to tell you I'm very sorry I was mean to you. I know I hurt your feelings."

Maggie says, "You did, Anna."

Then I see a slow grin.

"Actually, it was a good thing. It gave me a jolt. I started to think maybe you were right. At least I have a mother. Even if she wasn't my real mother, she's here."

"I shouldn't have said that. I'm sorry, Maggie."

"It was okay, because it shocked me and I realized I should stop whining about being adopted. I should ask her... so I did!"

"That was brave." I move closer to her on the bed.

"It happened when Mom asked me to make a pie with her. We were sitting waiting for the pie to bake, and I finally asked her. Mom looked surprised. She got out my birth certificate, and it had our names and everything on it. Now I know for sure."

"Oh, Maggie, that's wonderful."

"We had a good talk. Actually, we're a lot alike in many ways. Mom's not perfect, but hey, neither am I!"

She does look happier. It reminds me how different my own life would be if Mama were alive. Bella and the girls would still be with us.

Maggie puts her hand on my arm. "Something else, Anna. I've been afraid you might think it was my dad who had your sisters taken away."

I shake my head. "I never thought that, Maggie. My father and Mrs. Covey talked it over, and it was Papa's idea to go to the Welfare Department. He said he felt badly seeing me so worn out and was worried that *all* his girls were in trouble. The little girls, Bella, and *me*, as well."

"So you never blamed my father?"

"Not for a minute. Are we still friends then?"

"Of course we are. Best friends," Maggie says, squeezing my hand.

I squeeze back. "I wasn't sure. Carolyn said Jerry was your best friend now."

"Oh, Carolyn is jealous of us. She'd like to be best friends with me, but she never will be. I feel kind of sorry for her. I'm going to try and be nicer to her. It will be an effort!"

Anna smiles. "I'll be your partner for that project."

"Partner, and best friend too. Jerry *is* my friend, and he's fun to be with, but I'd never talk to him about the things you and I talk about. You can only have one *best* friend."

I smile at her, thinking that the one lucky thing in my life is having Maggie for my best friend.

And the worst thing is that I don't have Bella any more.

"I miss Bella so much, Maggie. I didn't have a chance to tell those people that she can't fall asleep unless you jiggle her in your arms. I keep looking at her empty cradle and I can't stop crying. Sometimes I cry the whole night."

Maggie puts her arm around me.

"Papa says that I *am* keeping my promise to Mama because I let Bella go to a family who can give her a better future than we could. I guess in a way he's right. But it feels as if those people have taken my place."

Maggie says, "Those people wanted a baby very badly. Remember they brought a knitted bonnet and jacket."

"I know. And they were very gentle taking her out to the car. But they'll *never* love Bella as much as I do."

Maggie shifts on the bed. "You told me you can visit Helen and Lucy."

"Yes, I see them a lot. They have matching bedspreads on the beds. Chenille, if you can believe it! Mrs. B, they call the woman. She brought each of them a doll with lots of doll clothes."

"Let me come with you to see Helen and Lucy. School ends in two weeks. We can take the girls everywhere in town this summer."

"I'm lucky to be part of their lives, but I don't call Mrs. B their foster mother. I call her 'foster person.'"

"I'll call her that too." Maggie smiles gently at me.

Then she says, "But now I'm worried about something else. It's my relationship with Dad. Ever since I stole the cigarettes, things haven't been right with us."

"What do you mean, Maggie?"

"I think every time he looks at me, he remembers I lied to him. He says he can never trust me. He never calls me Mags anymore."

Maggie's mother comes to the door and invites me to stay for lunch.

"Please stay, Anna," Maggie says. "We can see the girls together this afternoon."

"I've got until four, when I'm meeting my father."

Maggie's mother shows me where to sit at the lunch table. Tommy and her father are there too. Tommy starts to tell a knock-knock joke, but Maggie stops him. It doesn't bother him. He just keeps stuffing a peanut butter sandwich in his mouth and grinning at the same time. There's peanut butter stuck to the front of his teeth.

"Maggie tells us you've worked hard to catch up on your school work, Anna," her father says.

"Miss Alexander says I'll pass into grade eight for sure."

Her father smiles. "It's hard to believe you and Maggie will be in high school next year."

Maggie's mother's smiling too. "And I'm glad you'll have time with the girls this afternoon."

"Can I come?" Tommy asks.

Maggie looks at me and says, "It's up to Anna."

"Why not?" I tell Tommy. "Helen's almost your age. We'll go to the park and you can push Lucy on the swing."

Her mother gives me a bag with raisin cookies. "For you and your sisters," she says. "Maybe take some to the boys."

Maggie cuffs Tommy on the arm. "No jokes."

WEDNESDAY, JUNE 16

I NEED TO talk to Dad. I know what I have to say. Just *do* it!

I find him reading the paper. "Can we go somewhere private to talk sometime, Dad?"

He gives me a puzzled look. "Okay. How about today? I'll show you a favourite place of mine."

It's a little sudden, but I've been rehearsing what I want to say. I should be ready.

Dad leads the way up the trail heading west behind the barracks. He doesn't say a word, and neither do I. We climb the hill to the level part at the top, where Dad holds two strands of the barbed wire apart for me to duck through. I do the same for him.

We hike until we come to a huge boulder almost as tall as I am. It's the only big stone in the field. It has a rough top but is completely flat on one side. Dad runs his hand along the side and I do the same. It's worn as smooth as ice.

"People around here call this the buffalo stone. It's made of white granite," he says. "See where the buffalo have stamped down the dirt around it?"

I decide not to tell him that the correct name is bison.

Dad leans back against the stone. He looks out across the field and says, "This is an important place for me. When I come here, I think of the wild herds that travelled on this land. For hundreds of years those powerful creatures stopped to rub their backs against this stone. It must have made them feel good."

We stand, just the two of us on the hill, the sky so big behind us. I raise my head and see myself reflected in my father's sunglasses. I look like a small trembling gopher in the field.

Do it.

Here goes. "Dad, I'm sorry I stole the cigarettes. I know when an adult steals they end up in jail. I don't want to end up in one of those cells downstairs."

He smiles. "Certainly be easy for me to visit!"

"Dad! Not funny. So . . . I'm promising I won't ever, ever steal anything again."

"Good."

"And I promise not to smoke."

"I thought you liked the cigar?"

"Not much. Well, not at all."

I see the start of Dad's lopsided grin. "Figured that," he says. "Remember the feeling the next time you think about smoking."

We're both leaning back against the buffalo stone now, watching the wind ripple the grass across the field. It's like a painting of waves on the ocean.

Dad says, "It's easy for kids to get confused about things. If you're worried about something, ask your parents. We're here to help you."

"Do you mean like thinking I was adopted?"

"Yes. How could we possibly know you were thinking about that?"

"I'm glad I got up my courage to ask Mom."

"I can't imagine why you thought you were adopted. If you think about it, you are definitely our child. You've got your mother's quick temper, and you get your stubbornness from me. You certainly weren't going to let me know the cigar made you sick, were you?"

"I barely made it to the bathroom!" I confess. "But Dad, who do I *look* like? I don't look the same as either of you."

Dad laughs. "Don't you know?"

"No, I don't."

"You're so like your grandmother. I think of her every time I look at you."

I guess maybe I am like Gram. I have freckles on my nose and she had them on the back of her hands, and she wore glasses to read, even though I need them for everything. We both liked to sit and talk, and we both loved to laugh.

"What colour was Gram's hair before it turned white, Dad?"

"A nice warm brown, just like yours."

He bends to pick a stem from the green sage bush growing at the side of the rock and hands me some small leaves. I watch him crush the leaves between his fingers. I crush mine and sniff the healing spiciness again and again. I can't get enough of it.

Dad puts his arms around me and hugs me hard.

"One more thing, Dad," I say, staying close to him.

"Yes?"

"I think we should get Tommy a puppy. He really wants one."

"Not a bad idea. Let me talk to your mother."

"Tommy's already picked out a name."

"What is it?"

"He wants to call his dog Mickey Mouse."

Dad starts to laugh, and then I laugh, and the two of us can't stop.

"Time to go home, Mags," Dad says. He keeps his arm around my shoulders all the way back across the field and down the hill to the barracks.

Anna

TUESDAY JULY 6

MAGGIE AND I spent the morning with the girls at the children's swimming pool. It was fun to have Tommy along with us.

Now Maggie and I are back on the barracks lawn with a picnic lunch her mother made.

"I like your new glasses, Maggie," I tell her.

"I do too. I think they suit me better than the old ones," Maggie says. "Yesterday when Jerry and I went for a bike ride, he said that some girls look cute in glasses. You don't suppose he meant *me*!" She makes one of her funny faces.

Then she adds, "Jerry and I want you to come biking with us. You can use his mother's bike."

"That would be fun as long as I can see the girls first," I tell her. "I'm still part of their lives. Lucy's talking more, did you notice? And Helen's hair is easier to manage since Mrs. B cut it shorter."

"Mrs. B seems okay," Maggie says.

"You mean Misbee! Berny came to visit the other day. The girls hung onto his knees the whole time. Dad says maybe I can bring them to the farm for the day. Why don't you come too? The Saskatoon berries will be ripe in a few weeks."

"It's a deal," Maggie says.

"When the girls are older and in school, I want them to come back to live with us on the farm."

"So Mrs. B would be their foster person for only a few years until they're both in school?" Maggie asks.

"I hope it works that way. This whole thing has changed our family. Dad's around more, and he makes the boys do work around the house. Joe's got a part-time job at the service station now, and Papa lets him drive me in to town."

"And we've got high school in the fall! You worked so hard to pass this year."

"Miss Alexander said she was proud of me. And guess what, Maggie? She's invited me to bring the girls over to her house for lemonade next week."

"I think Miss Alexander has a soft spot for you," Maggie says.

"Do you? She gave me one of her books, *Anne of Avonlea*, and I'm reading it now. It's about Anne's first teaching job in Avonlea, when she helps two orphans."

Then without warning the empty feeling comes again. "But Maggie, I still miss Bella so much. At night my arms ache to hold her. I can hardly stand it. She's growing up out there somewhere. Without *me*. I'll never see her again."

I lie back on the grass and close my eyes.

Maggie sits quietly beside me for a long time, and then I hear her say, "I have an idea."

I sit up. "What is it? Tell me."

"Anna, when we're both grown up, let's go on a search. A search to find Bella."

It makes my head spin. Just thinking that some day I could find Bella. "Do you honestly think we could?"

"Sure we can."

"But we don't know where Bella is. It would cost a lot of money to travel around until we find her."

"We can do it, Anna. When we're older we can work and save money. We can travel all over the United States. We can cross the oceans and search all over the world if we have to. We'll find your sister!" Maggie's eyes are sparkling so much it looks like the freckles are dancing on her nose.

I feel my heart racing. "How old do you think we'd have to be?"

"Nineteen, maybe. Whenever we're ready to start looking. Let's just *do* it. Let's promise."

"I do promise," I say.

Maggie grabs my hands and looks me in the eye. "I promise, too."

And suddenly, my arms feel lighter. Maybe Bella isn't lost to me forever.

I run my hand over the grass, looking at the clover. Then at the same spot again. "Maggie! Here's a *four*-leaf clover!"

We leap to our feet, link hands, and start twirling around.

"We're going to be lucky. We *will* find Bella!" I say.

For the first time since Bella was taken away, I believe I might see my little sister again. I'll tell her about Mama and the rest of us who love her. I'll remind her how I rocked her through the long nights until the sky lightened.

At home I have the *Bluebird of Hope* Maggie gave me. That little bird will give me hope through the years until we start to look for Bella. I throw my arms around my wonderful friend.

"Thank you, Maggie. Thank you for everything."

One thing I know for sure is that we'll keep our promise. If it takes until we're old and grey, Maggie and I will search the world. We'll find Bella. She's out there somewhere, growing up happy, I hope.

We'll find her and we'll tell her about us.

Author's Note

THIS BOOK WAS inspired by the true story of a family in a small Saskatchewan town very like Deep Creek. As in the book, the mother of the family died in childbirth and the oldest girl promised to look after the baby, who was called Belle. The children were heartbroken when their sister was taken away from the family, but when they were grown, they began a long search for her.

In real life and after many false leads, they found their sister through the Salvation Army, but by then Belle was almost sixty years old. She had been living in the eastern United States and was happily married with three children of her own. Her American parents had never told her she was adopted, so it was a big surprise for her to learn that she had a large family in Saskatchewan. Sadly, Belle's birth father and her oldest brother had died by the time she was found. Her oldest sister, who had cared for her in those early months, was the first person to meet her. She arranged for Belle to travel to Canada and visit the rest of her family. At the joyful reunion, the family said, "We knew right away she was one of us."

Belle told them it made her feel guilty to think that her birth had caused them to lose their mother. They told Belle they had never blamed her. They took their sister to the farm where she'd been born and to visit her mother's and father's graves. Belle came back to Canada for many more happy visits with her family.

I met this family when I was writer-in-residence at the Wallace Stegner House in Eastend, Saskatchewan. I knew that someday I wanted to write about the young girl's experience.

I also wanted to capture the feeling of prairie life in the 1940s. The story is set in a fictional town in rural Saskatchewan and includes a lot of cigarette smoking. Young readers should be aware that adults didn't know then about all the health risks of smoking. They did know it was unhealthy for children to smoke.

Acknowledgements

MANY THANKS TO Frances and Tom Jenkins, who know all about red-tailed hawks and coyotes; Isabel Nuttall and Marylyn Eckart, who inspired me with their family story; Donny White, who shared his love of prairie stories; Linda Bailey, who taught me to keep my sentences short and much more; Norma Charles, who reminds me to have heart in the story; Dianne Woodman, for teaching me patience; Louise Hager, whose father made her smoke a cigar; Susan Moger, always my first reader; and my grandson Misha, who has good ideas.

Thanks to friends who support me as a writer: Debbie Hodge, Shirley Rainey, Dorell Taylor, Dana Brynelsen, Jinny Hayes, Susan Harris, Bob Heidbreder, Sheena, Victoria and Moira Koops, Harriet Zaidman, Jane Flick, Bob Harvey, Roberta Rich, Penny Perry, Andrea Harvey, and Pamela Porter.

Thanks for editing help to Katie Wagner, Tara Gilboy, Kathryn Cole, Kathy Stinson, and Arthur Slade.

I am grateful to Heritage House for seeing the possibility in this story: Lara Kordic, Leslie Kenny, Lenore Hietkamp, Lesley Cameron, and Setareh Ashrafologhalai.

About the Author

R. BLISSETT

BERYL YOUNG is the author of seven critically acclaimed books for children. She writes novels, biographies, and picture books, including *Wishing Star Summer*, *Charlie: A Home Child's Life in Canada*, *Would Someone Please Answer the Parrot!*, and *Follow the Elephant*. Among many award nominations, her books have won the Silver Moonbeam Medal (US), the Reader's Choice Award at the Rainforest of Reading, and the Chocolate Lily Award.

Beryl was born in Saskatchewan, where she lived for a year on her grandparents' farm and attended a one-room country school. She lives in Vancouver now, and while she loves the ocean and the mountains, a big part of her still yearns for those rolling prairie fields. For more information, visit berylyoung.com.